THE F

When she arrived in Darwin to visit
her fiancé Howard, Kate was disappointed to find that he was away
temporarily, and instead she was
obliged to spend most of her time with
his colleague Grig Jacobsen. And while
she waited, Kate found herself making
new discoveries about Howard—and
about herself . . .

THE RED SARONG

BY

RENA YOUNG

MILLS & BOON LIMITED
15–16 BROOK'S MEWS
LONDON W1A 1DR

First published 1983
Australian copyright 1983
Philippine copyright 1984
This edition 1984

© Rena Young 1983

ISBN 0 263 74722 0

Set in 10 on 11 pt Monophoto Plantin
01-0884 – 48855

*Made and printed in Great Britain by
Richard Clay (The Chaucer Press) Ltd,
Bungay, Suffolk*

CHAPTER ONE

THE Northern Territory heat hit Kate like a sledgehammer as she stepped off the plane at Darwin Airport. Her new, crisp cotton dress was a wet rag by the time she had crossed the tarmac to the barnlike terminal building. She was pleased that she'd put her dark hair up for the trip. Even so, perspiration ran in rivulets down her back, collecting and soaking her dress at the waist.

It was four o'clock Territory time. Howard should have been off duty and there to meet her. But she couldn't see him anywhere. She spent a few minutes carefully perusing the crowd milling about the building, before asking at the information desk where to pick up her luggage. Frustrated and angry that he should leave her in this predicament in a strange place, she bustled out of the terminal to the baggage area to find her cases—only to find that the more she hurried, the more hot and sticky she became.

The baggage was on an airline trolley at the side of the building and passengers were crowded round it, grabbing suitcases and bags willy-nilly, with no apparent supervision. Hers didn't seem to be there, and tears of rage began to fill her eyes.

'Looking for these, Miss Rhodes?' came a deep, rich voice from behind her. Kate whirled in confusion to see a tall, Naval officer, resplendent in tropical whites, grinning at her obvious discomfort with her luggage sitting like traitors at his feet.

'Lieutenant Grigor Jacobsen reporting for duty, ma'am,' he said, snapping a mocking salute. 'Lieutenant Monroe sends his regrets,' he continued in a drawl, 'and has asked me to see that you're settled in.'

'What's happened to Howie?—I mean Lieutenant Monroe?' asked Kate, a little shakily. Her anger subsided as she realised she wasn't to be left in an alien place to fend for herself.

'Unfortunate change of plans,' replied her Naval companion, guiding her by the elbow to a tiny red sports car, parked nearby in a 'No Parking' zone, and throwing her bags, like so much junk, into the back. Kate's hackles rose. There was some fragile stuff in her gear and she objected to it being thrown around. Her escort didn't seem to notice her dismay as he ushered her into the front seat and sped off at an alarming rate.

'Howard's boat had to take the T.I. patrol at the last minute,' he shouted over the roar of the wind.

'T.I.?' yelled Kate questioningly, as she tried to keep her hair in place. The least he could have done, she mused to herself, was to have supplied a scarf!

'Sorry. Thursday Island,' came the reply, wafting past her in the slipstream.

Kate lapsed into silence, deciding any questions she had could wait till they reached their destination, wherever that was.

She settled back to enjoy the relative coolness that the speeding car afforded. It seemed only moments before the little car zoomed into the parking area of a block of flats and her escort was pulling her cases out.

'Home, ma'am, at least for now,' he said, opening her door for her and indicating with a nod that she was to follow him.

She did, in silence, admiring the back view of his well assembled body, clad in brilliant white shirt and shorts which showed off his muscular legs to perfection.

She shook herself mentally as she became aware of what she was doing, reminding herself that she was an engaged girl—well, woman—and that Howard was exactly what she wanted in a husband. No pair of legs, no matter how muscular, should be taking up so much of her thoughts. Unless, of course, they were Howard's.

'Here we are.' The voice interrupted her thinking and she came back to earth to find he'd opened the door to a flat on the second floor. He stood aside to let her in and followed with her baggage, together with an overnight bag that she didn't recognise.

'That bag isn't mine!' Kate cried in alarm. 'Someone off the plane will think they've lost it. We'll have to take it back!'

'No problems,' the giant blond replied. 'It's mine. I live here and this is just some washing I've brought home from the boat.' He burst out laughing as he saw the look of consternation on Kate's elfin face. 'Obviously, Howard hasn't told you,' he continued through his laughter. 'We share this place when we're not at sea. Though usually we're here separately. You see, when I'm in, Howard's out and vice versa. You can have his room for now and make sleeping arrangements to suit yourselves when Howard comes ashore.'

'When will that be?' asked Kate, ignoring the implication that she and Howie would automatically share a bed when he returned.

'Can't wait for him to get back, eh?' he quipped with a gleam in his wicked blue eyes that let her know he was thinking the worst. 'Sorry to disappoint you. He'll be gone for at least ten days, so you'll have to pinch-hit with me till then. I'm completely at your service, and prepared to accommodate you in any way,' he added with a leer.

Grabbing her bags, Kate was about to flee from this infuriatingly arrogant man, only to find he was faster on his feet than his bulk suggested and he was barring the door with his body.

'Look, I'm only teasing,' he said in a voice full of apology. 'Howard led me to believe you could take a joke, and I was only joking. I know you must be disappointed that he wasn't here to meet you, but it can't be helped. I did promise him I'd look after you till he got back.' Gently he removed the bags from her hands. 'My friends call me Grig. Friends?' he asked, apparently subdued.

'I don't seem to have much choice, do I?' quavered Kate, tears spilling uncalled from her almond-shaped, hazel eyes.

'I really am sorry, Kate. I can call you Kate,

can't I? I can't keep calling you Ma'am,' he asked repentantly, as he tried to wipe the tears from her face with a starched white handkerchief. It refused to blot them up and caused Kate's sense of humour to surface as the starch scratched her cheek.

'I suppose you'll have to, if we're going to be living together,' she replied, bursting into uncontrollable giggles, that gave way to hysterical laughter.

'You know what your trouble is,' said Grig seriously. 'You're suffering from jet-lag and heat. Sit down, for God's sake, woman, while I make you a drink.'

Kate sat down with relief in one of the cane armchairs and began to relax. Looking round her, she became aware that the flat was rather tastefully decorated with a bright floral motif in the curtains and chair covers.

The front door led directly into the main room, which had a set of french windows leading to a balcony. Beside them was a cane room divider which doubled as a kitchen bench, and behind that, out of view to anyone, was the kitchen. Two doors led off the living area to the left and she knew these must be the bedrooms. But where was the bathroom? Kate felt hot and uncomfortable. A shower and change of clothes might help get things back into perspective. The sounds of Grig pottering about in the kitchen brought her again to the problem at hand.

'Where's the bathroom?' she called. 'I think it would help if I had a shower.'

He appeared round the corner, and by the look

on his almost too-handsome face, she knew she was in for more of his teasing.

'These flats are new and we have en-suites, almost,' he chuckled, opening the farthest door to the left. He ushered her into a spacious bedroom, sparsely furnished with just a double bed, dressing table and built-in robes.

'This is Howard's room—well, yours now. The bathroom's through here.' He opened a door and showed her a large modern bathroom.

'This is my lair,' he told her, crossing the bathroom and opening another door directly opposite it with a flourish. Kate caught a glimpse of a small, tidy single room.

'There *is* a lock on this door to stop anyone barging in unannounced,' he said with a lopsided grin. 'You'd better lock it now so I don't catch you in the altogether. But remember to unlock it when you've finished or I'll have to come through your room to use the ablutions. That,' he emphasised, 'can be embarrassing—as Howard and I have found from bitter experience. Clean towels in the cupboard,' he called through the already closed door.

Wondering exactly what he meant by the last remark about bitter experience, Kate returned to her own room, to find her bags on the bed. She hadn't seen Grig put them there and knew she must be in a worse state than she'd imagined.

'Pull yourself together,' she commanded herself. 'You're supposed to be on holiday to relax and enjoy yourself, and a fine start you've made! The least little thing goes wrong and you go to pieces. So Howie wasn't here to meet you. You'll have to get used to that sort of thing, my girl, if you want to be a navy wife.'

She pulled clean clothes angrily from her suitcase and, still muttering to herself as she collected her toilet articles, took herself off to the shower.

The cold water beating down on her cream skin shook the cobwebs from her brain and made the world look a little less harrowing. This friend of Howard's would take some getting used to, she told herself. He was so unlike anyone she'd ever met before.

Smiling to herself as she lathered with the new bathsoap she had bought especially for the trip, because of its fragrance, she wondered if he was always as arrogant and infuriating as he had been with her, or if it was some sort of façade. The thought crossed her mind that it would be interesting if he were always like that. After all, she mused, it isn't every day a girl gets a chance to deal with a real live Rhett Butler type, and it might even be fun to try for a couple of days. She chuckled as she thought of the prospect and her mood lightened.

She entered the living room a few minutes later and found Grig sitting sprawled in an armchair, a frosty beer glass, almost empty, in his hand. He eyed her with what she felt was more than passing interest, and she pulled at her blouse awkwardly.

'That feels much better,' she said hesitantly. 'I really must apologise for my behaviour before. I'd been so looking forward to seeing Howie again, I think disappointment got the better of me. The heat didn't help either,' she added, lamely. He was still appraising her and his silence was unnerving. 'I was warned about it, but it was worse than I'd imagined. Forgiven?' She grinned a little sheepishly.

'Will you please stop staring at me. You make me nervous,' she blurted, after another moment of silence.

'Sorry,' Grig apologised. 'But the change is rather remarkable. A grown-up woman goes into my shower and a half-grown waif emerges. It's supposed to work the other way round—or so all the stories go.'

Kate giggled with delight and congratulated herself on choosing to change into shorts and to leave her long dark hair loose. She knew that without make-up, as she was now, and without her high-heeled shoes, she did look rather young. It had something to do with her height. At only just five feet, it was difficult at times to convince people of her true age and she sometimes played on it.

'Now don't start getting hysterical again,' Grig warned, as Kate continued to laugh at him. 'Here, have a drink. Maybe that will settle you down. God help him if that bastard Monroe has saddled me with a female who gets hysterical at the drop of a hat!'

Kate stopped abruptly. She wasn't sure if he were serious or not. But the look in his blue eyes seemed to tell her he was joking.

'How dare you call Howard a bastard?' she demanded, trying to sound angry, but she only succeeded in letting him know that she was now functioning normally and had accepted his remark in the spirit it was intended.

'I'll call him more than that when I see him. He told me you were grown up, and now I find he's been cradle-snatching.' His eyes twinkled.

'If you like, I can go in and put my hair up and do my face,' said Kate, twisting her hair and holding it on top of her head.

They both laughed and the atmosphere relaxed. Kate sipped her drink tentatively. It was a pale pink concoction and the flavour was somehow familiar.

'What is this?' she asked.

'The Jacobsen cure-all for heat exhaustion. Crushed ice, Campari and lemonade—very refreshing.' They sat in companionable silence for a while, till Grig put down his beer glass and stretched.

'Now that you're behaving like a human being,' he said, 'I might be able to change out of this monkey suit into something more comfortable ... I know that's supposed to be the woman's line,' he added, with a wicked grin, 'but here in the tropics, we've got men's as well as Women's Lib. If you like sunsets,' he added, vanishing into his own room, 'You'll see a great one from the balcony. You can see Fanny Bay from there and the sea looks great at sunset.'

Kate took his advice and wandered out, drink in hand, to the balcony. The sun had almost set and the dying rays lit up the sea, turning the bay to blood sea. Low black clouds sat on the horizon like pillows edged in gold. She had never seen such a breathtaking sunset and she determined to be up early to see if the sunrise was as magnificent.

She was still standing, stunned, when a soft noise behind her brought her back to reality. Grig had come up behind her and was standing watching her. She was surprised to see that he wore only a sarong, tied at the waist and sweeping the floor Fijian style. She raised her eyebrows, but bit back the exclamation that rose to her lips.

Instead she asked quietly, 'Darwin rig?' He nodded agreement.

It certainly looked cool and comfortable and she found herself, much to her own amusement, admiring the shape of his body—tall, over six feet in height, and slim, but completely in proportion. He reminded her of the statues of Greek athletes she'd seen in museums. The sarong on someone else might have seemed an affectation, but on him it was perfect. She wondered what she would look like herself in one and decided to buy one as soon as possible to try it. After all, she thought, when in Rome.

'I had planned to take you out for a meal tonight when I found I was to be playing host,' Grig began, 'but I finally decided that you'd probably like to get squared away and have an early night after your long flight. Sydney to Darwin in one day is a bit of a drag, I know. We could eat out if you like,' he finished lamely. His bantering tone of before was gone.

'I do think an early night is a good idea,' Kate told him. 'Besides, neither of us is exactly dressed for dining out, are we?' She deliberately kept her tone light so he would know that they were starting on a new footing.

Grig was quick to pick up the tone and with obvious relief said, 'I suppose I'll have to think about something for dinner, then.'

'I don't mind cooking. That is if there is anything to cook in a bachelor pad,' Kate said quickly, eager to keep their new-found friendliness alive.

'You're my guest, ma'am,' he told her, 'and though I may not be a Cordon Bleu chef, my baked beans on toast have to be tasted to be believed! You'll sit right here while I take care of the cooking,' he finished. Then he smiled his lopsided smile again and any tension that had been lingering between them vanished. 'Mind you,' he added, 'house rules say that if you don't cook, you do the washing up.'

'Oh, do they? Well, I'll just have to take over the cooking while I'm here, then, won't I?'

'House rules also say that when a woman takes over my kitchen, she does the lot,' Grig told her, laughing. 'Anyway, the house rules are suspended for tonight, so just sit back and enjoy the breeze and I'll even bring you another drink while I fix us something to eat.'

He was as good as his word, and with the long cool drink in her hand, Kate sat back to contemplate the sea, stars and Howard, in the velvety tropical night.

She wondered what her holiday with Howard was to become. It certainly hadn't started too well and she really had given Grig a hard time—a hard time he didn't deserve. After all, he had only been trying to do a favour for a friend and she'd been behaving as if everything were his fault.

He was very attractive, she thought, but really not her type at all. She couldn't imagine him being tender and thoughtful the way Howard had always been with her. He appeared so forceful. But was that necessarily a bad thing? she wondered. His wife would never have to worry about making decisions. He was the type that would decide everything. She was being unfair. After all, she mused, I don't know him well enough to make those judgements.

Still turning over in her mind the enigma that was Grig Jacobsen, Kate drifted off to sleep, exhausted by the heat and the excitement of her day.

She stirred. Someone was whispering. 'It's time to eat.' But she was too tired to wake up. Her eyes flickered as she felt two strong arms pick her up from the chair, then opened fully in fright.

'It's all right,' Grig's now familiar voice penetrated her sleep-filled brain. 'You fell asleep and I was just going to put you to bed.'

The fright left her eyes as she realised what was happening. 'But you promised me baked beans,' she complained, 'and I'm starving!'

Grig deposited her, none too gently, on one of the armchairs in the living room. A gateleg table had been set up near the balcony, so that it was possible to open the balcony doors to their fullest and have the semblance of dining under the stars. Candles burned in wine bottles on the divider, a frost-dewed carafe of wine glistened in the middle of the table.

'Dinner is served, even though milady isn't exactly dressed for the occasion,' said Grig, smiling at Kate's rumpled appearance. Her blouse had come adrift from her shorts while she slept, and she hastily adjusted it.

'If I'd known you were going to go to this amount of trouble, I'd have put on an evening gown, but I don't have one to match your evening wear,' she responded in kind.

He pulled out her chair and helped her to the table, where a particularly tempting-looking prawn cocktail, with prawns too big to be believed, set her mouth watering and reminded her that she had hardly eaten all day. She'd been too excited. Grig sat opposite her and poured them each a glass of the freezing wine.

'Tell me about you and Howard,' he demanded, between mouthfuls.

Kate bridled at his tone, decided it was probably just his manner and ignored it. 'There isn't really much to tell,' she said. 'We've known each other for years. Howard was in school with my brother Peter in Adelaide. Pete brought him home to Sydney one Christmas and it went from there. We wrote for a while, till Howard came to Sydney to join the Navy and we spent most of his off duty time together. We just sort of grew into love, I guess,' she said, rather wistfully. 'We decided to become engaged when he was sent here. We probably would have married sooner, but after I'd finished my nursing, I'd started a Uni course in business administrations and I wanted to finish it.'

'Doesn't sound too romantic to me,' Grig commented, picking up the empty cocktail dishes and carrying them to the kitchen.

'Well, it was,' Kate answered defiantly, sounding as though she was trying to convince herself as well as Grig. Put like that, she thought to herself, it doesn't. But that isn't any of his business.

'We had some great times before he came to Darwin and he's really wonderful fun to be with,' she continued aloud.

'Yes, he would be. From a woman's point of view, that is,' answered Grig, depositing an enormous steak in front of her, complete with a crisp side salad.

'You don't think I'll eat all that?' Kate asked in amazement. She wondered what he meant by 'a woman's point of view'. 'Anyway, you promised me baked beans,' she smiled, trying to make up for the gaucheness of her remark.

'Sorry—wasn't thinking. But you'll have to get used to this. Up here it's usually too hot to eat much during the day. Most folk have their main meal, and a big one at that, at night when it's cooled off,' explained Grig, by way of apology.

'I guess there's a lot I've got to learn about Darwin. Since we're friends now,' said Kate with a wry smile, 'I hope you'll help me.'

'Of course I will. What are friends for? How's the steak?'

She was a little bewildered by the sudden change that came over Grig. His eyes had darkened, she noticed, and she wondered why her request for his help should cause any problems.

'The steak's delicious. You really can cook, can't you?' she told him.

'Just one of my many talents,' he replied. He seemed relieved to be on safer topics of conversation.

'As a matter of fact, my coxswain has started a scheme on board where everyone has a go at cooking now and then. It gives the chef a day off occasionally when we're away for a couple of weeks. It's surprising how many of the crew can knock up a reasonable meal when they want to. Those that can't are beginning to get their wives and girl-friends to teach them how to make something so they won't be left out.'

'I'll bet you get some extraordinary meals at times.'

'You're not wrong,' he grinned. 'One of the stokers comes from the Ukraine and he's written to his mother for some of her recipes. Another of the boys is from Thursday Island and he makes a pretty mean curry. I haven't asked my mother for any of hers yet. I'm waiting to see how cosmopolitan we get before I do that.'

'What do you mean?' Kate asked, a little bewildered.

Grig laughed. 'My mother is a bit of a character. One of her hobbies is cooking and I never know from one visit to the next what she'll be serving. Some of the things she dishes up wouldn't go down too well on board.'

'It can't be that bad surely,' Kate smiled. She found it hard to imagine him with a mother. He seemed so self-assured, like someone who had been born an adult. Somehow the picture of Grig being dependent on anyone, even as a child, was inconceivable.

'The cooking isn't so bad, it's just some of the dishes are a bit way out.'

'Have you cooked anything for them yet?' asked Kate.

'Yes. I make what is laughingly referred to as the Boss's stew,' he chuckled.

'The Boss?' queried Kate. 'I was under the impression that you and Howard were Captains of your ships. Surely they should call you Captain.'

'Boats, Kate, not ships. We're only lieutenants, even though we're the skippers, and the ships, as you call them, are only patrol boats. The crews have got round that by calling us "Boss"! Except when the brass is around, then they call us "sir". It works rather well.'

'Doesn't that make for a discipline problem?' she asked.

'On the contrary, it solves one. You see,' he explained, 'for most of us, this is our first command and we haven't been in the service too long, so we have to rely on our senior sailors like the coxswain and the buffer. They're generally old enough to be the fathers of the younger sailors and have served ten or twelve years longer than their so-called captains. It makes life a bit hard for them at times when they have to put us right on certain things. But most of the officers are aware of this and act accordingly,' he added. 'Damn it, I sound like a lecturer on naval procedure! I'll stop before I bore you to death. I would have thought

Howard would have told you most of this, though.'

'No, he hasn't. And no, I'm not bored. So go on. I really should know more about the Navy if I'm going to be a navy wife,' Kate said.

'Well, what would you like to know?'

'You've mentioned the coxswain a couple of times, so tell me about him,' she suggested.

'He's sort of like the boat's policeman. He's also the clerk, storekeeper and doctor, and he stands duty watches as well,' Grig told her.

'Sounds like a busy fellow,' Kate smiled.

'He is. My coxswain, for example, has served twenty years and is going to retire soon. I'm trying to convince him to sign on again. He's a damn good hand and I don't want the Navy to lose him. He's good at his job and worries about the crew's welfare. He's got a couple of the younger sailors out of strife that could have been very serious for them if it had gone through channels. They'll be sorry to see him go. He's always prepared to let people have a second chance, and it seems to work.'

'You seem to have a close relationship with your crew,' observed Kate.

'Yes, I guess I have. But you see, I came up through the ranks, as they say, so I know a few of the problems,' he explained.

'What does coming up through the ranks mean?'

'In my case, it means that I joined the Navy as an apprentice. Then after I'd finished that and became a Chief Petty Officer Engineer, I applied for officer's training and then went through that.

That makes me quite a bit older than the officers who went straight to officer's training.'

'How much older?' Kate asked.

'Inquisitive, aren't we?' he said, looking carefully at her. 'If you really must know, I'm thirty-two. So you can work it out for yourself. That *was* what the question was about, wasn't it?'

'No, it wasn't!' Kate declared, blushing furiously. He knew she would have been able to calculate his age from Howard's and the age gap. How could he know she had wanted to? And why, she asked herself, did she? He was laughing at her and she was cross with herself for letting it bother her.

'Your description of things is a little different from Howard's,' she said, trying to take the discussion back to safer ground. 'I got the feeling that the boat's captain was surpreme, at least on Howard's boat.'

'I think you'll find that each one differs. After all, the boats only have eighteen of a crew, and that includes the Captain and the Ex.O.,' he explained. 'Any personality clashes on board can be disastrous and each skipper has his own way of dealing with it.'

'What's an Ex.O.?' enquired Kate.

'Boy, you do have a lot to learn about the Navy!' Grig exclaimed. 'An Ex.O. is an executive officer, usually a sub-lieutenant just out of school. On a patrol boat, he's second in command. He's there to get practical navigational experience. The crews all call him Ex.'

'Then Howard must have done his navigation in Sydney,' Kate said thoughtfully. 'I know he came here to take command of one boat and then after a year was transferred to another.'

Grig looked perturbed. 'He must have, if that's what he told you.'

Apparently anxious to change the subject, he rose and removed the empty plates. 'You see,' he said, indicating her empty plate with a nod, 'you were hungrier than you thought. Help yourself to another glass of wine while I get the coffee.'

'Why don't you let me wash up while you get the coffee?' asked Kate.

'That's the best offer I've had all day,' he answered.

She followed him to the kitchen and ran the hot water into the sink while he started preparing the percolater.

'How did you come to be sharing a flat with Howard?' she asked, stacking the dishes in the sink.

'I took over the room from the guy who'd been here before. He was going south and asked me if I wanted it. I jumped at the chance. Flats are hard to come by in Darwin and if you do manage to get one, they cost the earth. Makes things hard on our sort of pay.'

'Oh!' Kate exclaimed, looking up at him from her suds. 'Howard told me that most Navy officers have some other income. He's got money from a trust set up for him by his father.' She felt the air chill and turned to see a steely look in his eyes.

'Some of us like to think we can live on what we earn,' he said flatly.

'I'm sorry,' Kate apologised, 'I didn't mean to

imply anything. It was thoughtless of me to
mention money. It must have sounded as though
I were prying,' she said sheepishly, concentrating
hard on the washing up.

'I suppose someone like you would take having
money as a prerequisite for anyone you're
interested in,' said Grig, in a strangely distant voice.

'Certainly not!' Kate retorted heatedly. 'I
wouldn't care if the man I loved was a pauper!'

Grig's laughter interrupted her and she spun
round to face him, showering him with soapsuds.
He laughed even harder.

'Don't you laugh at me! I meant it. If the man
I loved didn't have a penny, it wouldn't matter a
damn to me. We'd manage somehow.'

'Somehow I can't see you pinching pennies in a
garret. Anyway, the matter's pretty moot, isn't it?
You'd hardly move in the circles where you'd
meet many paupers,' he told her sarcastically.

'How would you know who I meet? You don't
even know me or where I come from.'

'That's true. But I do know Howard, and he's
not the sort to socialise with the lower classes. Or
maybe I've misjudged him,' added Grig, with
raised eyebrows and a quizzical expression on his
face.

'Maybe you have!' Kate stormed, turning back
to the sink so he couldn't see the red that
suffused her cheeks. Howard was an awful snob,
she knew, and it was one of the things she
disliked about him. There aren't many, she told
herself, and a person can't help how he was
raised. He has so many other good points, she
thought, and I know after we're married I'll be

able to show him how silly his attitude is to
people less well off than he is.

'Anyway,' she added crossly, 'it sounds to me
as if you're an inverted snob. Just because you
don't have money, you look down your nose at
anyone who does!' For some unknown reason,
her statement sent him off into fresh gales of
laughter.

'Why is it you find everything I say so damn
funny?' she demanded.

'It isn't you, it's me. I have a strange sense of
humour,' he gasped.

'Well, I wish you'd explain it to me,' snapped
Kate, rattling the dishes angrily, as she put them
away.

'Maybe I will some day, when the time is right.
But in the meantime, I wish you'd treat the
crockery with a bit more respect. It costs money
to replace.' He picked up the percolater and
coffee cups and carried them into the living
room, still chuckling to himself.

Wretched man! Kate thought, the way he's
acting you'd think he had some secret joke he
wasn't letting me in on. Well, he can have all the
secret jokes he likes! He won't get me to bite
again. I wonder what he meant by 'when the time
is right'? she mused. I'm bothered if I'll ask him,
he'll only laugh at me again, and I've had enough
of that for one night. Perturbed, she followed him
into the other room. His laughter had hurt more
than she was prepared to admit, even to herself,
and Kate had never been one to be hurt by
laughter, unless it was spiteful, and Grig's had
certainly not been that.

She found him sitting at the table, coffee cup in hand, deep in thought. 'Penny for them,' she said, pouring herself a cup.

'You'd never believe them. Not now at least,' said Grig, gazing at her reflectively.

'You're not going to start off on guessing games again, surely?' she said. She could have bitten off her tongue for allowing him to know she'd been guessing at the meaning behind his words in the kitchen.

'Guessing games are my favourite after-dinner entertainment,' he teased.

'Are they indeed? Well, you'll just have to play them by yourself tonight,' Kate told him. 'I'm going to bed.'

'An early night will do you good,' he said, looking a little concerned. 'You must be exhausted. I should have made you go to bed when you fell asleep. But somehow I don't think I could make you do anything.'

She was puzzled by his tone, but too tired to reflect on it.

'Goodnight,' she said. 'I'll see you in the morning.'

To her surprise he got up and took her by the shoulders. 'Goodnight, little girl,' he whispered, bending down to brush her cheek with his lips. 'Sleep tight.'

Kate's heart gave a strange little flutter and she had to restrain herself from touching her cheek where he'd kissed her. She looked into those laughing blue eyes and her heart bumped again. It took almost all her willpower to stop herself reaching up to touch his face. Quickly she turned on her heel and almost ran to the bedroom.

Inside she stood with her back to the door, heart racing and confused. How could someone she had just met affect her like this? He could hurt her by laughing at her. He could make her angry. He could even make her want him, and she'd only known him a few hours. He could even make her forget Howard.

Howard, Howard, why weren't you here? Why did you leave me to deal with this strange, exciting man?

Exciting! Why had she suddenly found him exciting? One fleeting kiss didn't mean anything, shouldn't mean anything. I won't let it mean anything, she promised herself.

She donned her nightdress, still confused, still feeling his lips on her cheek. She fell into bed, drained. She was exhausted and her mind and emotions were playing tricks on her. Tomorrow everything would be different. Tomorrow she'd be able to deal with him. Tomorrow, when she was herself again, she'd realise this was just reaction to the trip and the heat.

She drifted into a fitful sleep, her hair spread fanlike across the pillow. Her eyes flickered.

Someone was in her room. Through half closed eyes she saw Grig standing at the doorway looking at her, but she was too tired to move.

Still almost asleep, she saw him cross the room to enter the bathroom and vaguely she knew she must have forgotten to unlock the bathroom door.

'God damn you, Howard Monroe. God damn

you to hell.' The words drifted into her sleep-sodden brain and her mind said it was Grig's voice.

Almost immediately the words were forgotten and she was asleep.

CHAPTER TWO

KATE woke next morning to the sound of a deep, rich baritone singing one of the popular love songs of the day. At first she thought someone had a radio on, but the splashings that accompanied the voice told her that her new-found landlord-of-sorts was having his morning shower.

She felt uneasy, and something tugged at the back of her mind like an errand she had forgotten. The feeling was strong. There was something she should remember. But try as she might it wouldn't surface. To hell with it, she thought, if it's important enough, it will come back.

She stretched and bounced out of bed. Her brother Peter, she recalled, had always said she was too cheerful for her own good first thing in the morning. She wondered what Grig would be like in the morning, then guilt flooded her mind. I should be wondering what Howard will be like in the mornings, she reminded herself.

Howard! Now she remembered what was making her uneasy. Grig had thought her still asleep when he came through her room last night and she had heard him cursing Howard.

She wondered why. They were supposed to be friends, at least according to Howard. Why would Grig curse him? She decided to try to find out from Howard when he got back, and putting the incident from her mind she tied her hair in a ribbon and threw on a light robe.

Sauntering out to the kitchen, she revelled in the strong morning sunlight that flooded through the windows. The coffee pot was already full and hot and she poured herself a steaming mug of the fragrant brew. She carried it to the balcony and stood sipping it slowly as she watched the sea.

Grig burst out of his room towelling his hair, still singing. He didn't notice her silently watching him and he jumped when she asked sweetly, 'Sleep well?'

'You're up, are you? Hope I didn't wake you. I was going to let you sleep a bit longer,' he mumbled through the towel.

'Not really. But it is nice to waken to music.'

'You're nice and cheerful this morning. Ten hours' sleep has done you the world of good,' he said, pouring himself a mug of coffee. 'I'll have to remember that for the future. Then when you get stroppy on me, I'll know to put you to bed for ten hours or so.' His grin was infectious and they both laughed.

'I see you found the coffee,' he commented, lighting a cigarette.

'Could I have one of those?' Kate asked.

'You've already got one,' he answered, nodding at her coffee mug.

'I meant a cigarette. I ran out yesterday and meant to buy some at the airport. But in all the confusion ...' She trailed off and they both smiled, remembering their near-disastrous encounter the previous day.

'Didn't know you smoked,' he said, handing

her his packet and leaning over to light her cigarette.

'I don't much. Howard doesn't like it. But I enjoy one occasionally with coffee.'

'I'm trying to give the damn things up,' said Grig with a grimace.

'I lasted till you went to sleep last night. Hadn't smoked for nearly a week—shows what a bad effect you have on me. A couple of hours with you and I need something to steady my nerves!' He was trying to look angry, but with his hair uncombed and a towel around his shoulders, he just looked comical, and Kate laughed.

'Don't tell me the great Lieutenant Jacobsen has a character fault,' she mocked.

'Only two,' he said seriously, running his hand through his damp hair. 'One you've already discovered, and the other,' he rose to tower over her, 'is not being able to stand cheeky women first thing in the morning.'

He bent down to look into her eyes and Kate stepped back, unsure. Was he really serious? Then she caught the gleam in his eye.

'I *have* been known to spank them if they get too out of hand,' he threatened, and advanced on her, arms outstretched. But she eluded him and fled into her room to the sound of 'Chicken!' from behind her.

She felt pleased with herself as she dressed. They seemed to have started out on a friendly basis and she hoped they would be able to keep it that way. She had every intention of keeping things cool, but she was still a little unsure of Grig. She seemed to be able to make him angry so easily. Perhaps he'd been tired too yesterday. After all, he had been pressganged into baby-sitting a girl he knew nothing about and spending his valuable spare time looking after her.

It's up to me to fit in with his plans, she decided. When Howard returns, he can show me everything I want to see. So, Kate Rhodes, she told herself, no tears today, no moods, no teasing, just bright happy submission to anything His Lordship proposes. 'His Lordship'—yes, that fits him rather well. Kate smiled and humming softly went about her toilet.

She entered the living room, dressed for the day in a gay, autumn-toned print sundress. Her shoulders were bare and her hair fell in a long silken rope over her left breast. Her sandals were strappy and high, giving her more height, and she had added the bare minimum of make-up. A touch of green eyeshadow to accentuate her huge eyes, coppery-coloured lip-gloss, guaranteed to make any girl's lips kissable, (Kate had laughed at the ad, but liked the product) and a dash of her favourite cologne.

She watched him look her up and down. A strange feeling of satisfaction overcame her when she realised he approved of her outfit. She glowed involuntarily when he came close and sniffed. 'Very nice. Not one of my favourites, but it suits you.'

Breakfast had been set out on the divider—chilled pawpaw, toast and more coffee.

'Help yourself,' Grig told her, pouring the drinks.

Kate took a piece of the unfamiliar fruit and

found the orange flesh, drenched with lemon juice, delicious.

'What would you like to do today?' he asked between mouthfuls.

Remembering her resolve to be as little of a nuisance as possible, she said, 'What had you planned? There isn't much I have to do that couldn't wait.'

His eyes flashed with disgust, and Kate was startled. What had she said now?

'Look,' he said, 'when I ask a question, I expect a direct answer. Women who dither about trying to impress only annoy me. So, how about we start again? What would you like to do today?'

Regardless of her resolution, Kate found her anger hard to contain.

'I'm not one of your sailors!' she spat at him. 'There's no need to treat me like one!'

'Best we start the way we mean to go on,' he replied, his mouth twitching as he suppressed a smile.

'Does that mean you'll do anything I want?'

'No. All it means is that I expect you to tell me the truth when I ask a question. If it's possible and not too much trouble, then I'll fall in with your wishes.'

'If not?' she raised her eyebrows.

'If not, then you either do your own thing or put up with whatever it is I've planned. I'm not unreasonable.'

'Not unreasonable! You're impossible! All you have to say according to your set of rules is "It's too much trouble", and I get ruled out. I might as well not say anything,' Kate retorted heatedly.

'You could always spend the next few days in the flat by yourself till your precious Howard gets back,' said Grig.

'That isn't the first time you've been less than flattering to Howard,' Kate said angrily. 'What have you got against him? I thought you were supposed to be his friend.'

'I'm only sharing a flat with him,' he said, starting to clear away the breakfast things. 'What I think of Howard is my business.'

'That's typical!' she snarled. 'I have to tell you the truth, but you can opt out without any explanation. Do what you like. I'll stay here or find my own way about.'

I won't cry, I won't, she told herself, clenching her fists and squeezing her eyes shut to stop the tears from spilling.

Full of her own thoughts, Kate did not hear Grig come up behind her. 'Why do we always manage to strike sparks off each other?' he asked tenderly, touching her hair.

'There wouldn't be any sparks from me if you weren't so damn chauvinistic,' she muttered under her breath.

'We're only going to be thrown together like this for a short time,' he said, still touching her hair. 'Let's try and make the best of it. Shall we? I promise to try to control my male chauvinism.' Kate looked into his eyes to see if he was teasing her again, but he seemed to be serious, 'If you'll try not to take everything I say so damn seriously. Deal?'

'O.K. Deal,' she agreed with relief. Somehow the idea of not being with him was abhorrent.

'Now, what would you like to do today?' he asked, pouring himself another cup of coffee and sitting down beside her.

'Back to square one,' Kate laughed shakily. The feeling of inadequacy in his presence was strong and she suppressed it determinedly. 'I'd like to go shopping for a couple of things ... That is if it falls in with your plans.'

'Anything special you wanted?' he asked. The tension between them abating.

'I did want to see if I could find a couple of sarongs. I like yours and they seem to be the most suitable things to wear in this heat,' she told him, a little defensively.

'No problems. There are one or two shops that specialise in that sort of thing. In fact, you'll probably see quite a few women wearing them while we're out.'

'In the streets,' said Kate, amused.

'Sure. Things are very informal up here.'

Relief flooded her. They were back to a somewhat guarded friendship. But at least that was better than outright warfare. I'm beginning to think in military terms, Kate thought. Oh well, it might help with Howard. Why should I need any help with Howard? She twisted the ring on her left hand impatiently. I don't need any help with Howard. But at the moment I sure need some help with Grig. The thought was confusing.

'You'd better pull yourself together if you want to come shopping,' Grig's voice broke in and she realised she'd been in a world of her own—a world so confusing that she was happy to leave it and come back to reality.

'I'm ready,' she said, 'All I have to do is get my bag. Are you going like that?' She eyed his shorts, thongs and tee-shirt sceptically.

'Of course. This is normal Darwin shopping rig. I'd get laughed out of town if I dressed up here during the day.'

Kate hurried to the bedroom and found her handbag. As an afterthought, she caught up her cartwheel sunhat and she was ready.

As they left the flat, she noticed one of the female tenants watching them intently. 'Do you know her?' she asked.

'Oh, her. Yes. Looks like we've been sprung. She's the wife of one of Howard's crew. The coffee mornings will be nice and bright for a few days now.'

'What do you mean?' Kate asked, gracefully folding herself into the front seat of the tiny red car.

'You'll find out,' he said, and refused to be drawn further on the matter.

Choosing Kate's sarongs was an adventure in itself to her. She had never been clothes-shopping with a man before, and Grig's insistence that he knew better than she what would suit her came as á shock.

'Grig, I hate the green one, it's too bright, and the red one looks like something a street girl would wear,' she complained, when he told her in no uncertain terms which ones to buy.

'You obviously haven't seen any street girls lately,' he retorted. 'Something like this would be too conspicuous for them. Only nice girls would get away with it. Besides, the red one sets off your hair and the green one your eyes.'

'I think I'll take the cream one and the pale blue one,' Kate told the shop assistant.

'And I'll have those two,' Grig added, pointing to the red and green sarongs that Kate had refused. 'You can wear them for me at the flat,' he added loudly.

'Now look what you've done! She thinks we're living together,' Kate hissed, when the shop assistant gave her a knowing smile. 'Anyway, Howard would have a fit if he saw me in one of those. So you might as well save your money.'

'Why try to hide it, dear?' he said with an evil grin. 'Darwin is a very small town and everyone will find out we're living together sooner or later.' He winked at the shop girl, who returned the compliment, happy to have been allowed to join the conspiracy.

'Howard won't have to see you in them,' he said softly in Kate's ear. 'I bought them for my enjoyment, not his.'

The shop assistant handed them their parcels and Grig, smiling smugly, took Kate's arm and in a voice loud enough for everyone in the shop to hear said, 'Come along, darling, let's go straight home and see how you look in them.'

'Grig!' Kate hissed. 'Behave yourself! People are staring.'

'Let them—they're only jealous,' he told her, and with a satisfied chuckle escorted her from the shop.

By the time they returned to the car, Kate realised his actions in the shop had been meant, as they had, to shock her, and her happy-go-lucky mood returned. She was relaxed in Grig's

company for the first time since she had met
him, and she could see the humour in his
harassment of the poor shop assistant. Apart
from the outburst at breakfast, things had
settled down to a smooth, friendly relationship
and she found herself laughing with him much
as she would with her brother Peter. Something
in the back of her mind told her he would
never be like a brother to her and she pushed
the thought aside quickly, suppressing it, she
hoped, for all time.

'Want to see a patrol boat?' his voice broke into
her contemplations.

'I'd like that,' she said, wondering if there
would be many sailors around at the weekend.

'There won't be many of the crew around,' he
told her, reading her mind, 'so this is probably a
good time to see it. During the week it's a bit
hard to do the tourist bit without falling over
sailors.'

The little car turned a corner and sped down a
particularly steep hill, cornering savagely at the
bottom and speeding towards a boom gate. Kate's
heart was in her mouth. We're going to go right
under it, she thought, and ducked her head to
miss being decapitated.

Grig grinned at her discomfort as he screamed
the car to a halt inches from the gate. The figure
of a uniformed attendant appeared from inside
the glassed cubicle that reminded Kate of the toll
booths on the Sydney Harbour Bridge.

'You'll go right under that gate one day, mate,'
the attendant told Grig, in a not too-unfriendly
tone. He waved them through, raising the boom.

'He wasn't very deferential to your rank,' Kate said facetiously.

'Doesn't have to be, he's not Navy.'

The idea of civilians manning Naval establishments was surprising to Kate. She was used to seeing sailors on duty at the gates of the depots she'd visited in the South. 'Who is he, then?' she asked.

'He's employed by Harbours and Marines,' Grig explained. 'You see, Stokes Hill Wharf is the main one for Darwin and most incoming vessels tie up here. It isn't just the patrol boat landing. Causes problems at times when it's busy and all the crews want to park their cars close to the boats. The Harbour and Marine guys get a bit hot under the collar at times about it, but I get on fairly well with most of them.'

He parked the car hard against a warehouse and Kate was forced to climb out his side.

'These sort of cars have their advantages,' he smiled, and ushered her ahead of him to a flight of rusty metal stairs.

The tide was out and Kate hadn't seen the patrol boat that was anchored there. The tide was so low that the radar mast was the only thing visible above the wharf, and she didn't know what it was until Grig told her.

'I'd better go first from here to help you,' he said, taking her hand and escorting her up the gangway. 'You'll have to remember to wear low shoes when you come to the boats again.'

A solitary sailor was sitting in a deck chair holding a fishing line. Dressed only in shorts, he hurriedly donned his tee-shirt on Kate's appearance. She was surprised to see he was only about twenty and not very comfortable around women.

'Caught anything today, Dave?' Grig asked.

'Never get much around here, boss. Still, it helps to pass the time,' he said, shuffling his feet in embarrassment. 'If I'd known you were going to bring a visitor,' he added, 'I'd have got something ready for lunch. I could rustle up a couple of salads if you like.' He seemed anxious to leave them.

'Don't worry about it,' Grig replied. 'We won't be staying for lunch. A cup of coffee would be nice, though.'

'Coming right up,' the young sailor said, and fled.

Grig led Kate to the wardroom, which was a room not more than eight feet square almost totally filled with a table attached to the bulk-head, surrounded on three sides by bench-type seats. Above it were cupboards and bookcases and a porthole covered with bright blue curtains which matched the one that served as a door.

'Take a seat,' Grig ordered. Kate felt the change in him from self-assured man-about-town to Naval officer, used to being obeyed, and the change suited him.

The young sailor appeared with two steaming cups and placed them carefully on the table.

'My, you've made an impression. Dave's even managed to find saucers,' Grig remarked, and the sailor blushed.

'The 'Swain's officer of the day,' he said diffidently. 'He's down in the for'ard mess doing some paper work. Want me to tell him you're here, boss?'

'If you wouldn't mind, Dave. Just tell him I've someone I'd like him to meet.' Kate was surprised at the way Grig spoke to the young man. Polite, but with authority and from the look on the sailor's face, it was clear that Grig's manner was appreciated.

She sat sipping her drink and taking in her surroundings. It was amazing, she thought, how anyone could manage in such cramped quarters.

Reading her mind, Grig, who had been watching her reactions with an amused smile said, 'If you think this is cramped, you should see the rest of the accommodation! At least the officers have cabins as well. The senior sailors have to use their sleeping quarters for office space and the junior sailors are even worse off.'

An older man dressed in navy blue shorts and shirt knocked on the bulkhead outside the wardroom.

'Come in, Spike,' said Grig, acknowledging the sailor's presence. 'I'd like you to meet Miss Rhodes, Lieutenant Monroe's fiancée.'

'Pleased to meet you, Miss Rhodes,' he said in a friendly way.

'Please call me Kate,' she smiled.

'Spike, I was wondering if Sheila would have the time to take Kate under her wing next week. Kate will be here by herself otherwise.'

Kate's face showed her consternation and Grig hurried to reassure her. 'Sheila is Spike's wife, and since we'll both be away for a two-day patrol, I thought she'd be the best person to show you round.'

'I'm sure she won't mind,' Spike added. 'You

know Sheila loves to have someone to look after—comes from having the kids grown up and away.'

'You don't look old enough to have grown-up children,' Kate told the sailor.

'Depends what you term grown-up, I suppose,' he said. 'Our boy is seventeen and at Nirimba, the apprentice school for the Navy, and our girl is nineteen and in college in Brisbane. Sheila and I married pretty young. We're one of the lucky Navy couples—we survived.'

Kate was startled by his personal outburst and wondered why he had felt the need to enlighten her.

'If you'd like, boss,' said Spike, 'you could bring Kate to our place tomorrow night for tea. That way the girls can get to know one another and make some plans.'

'That's a good idea. Want us to bring anything?' Grig asked.

'Just the usual, thanks, boss. I'll leave you to it and see you both tomorrow. Nice to meet you, Kate.'

'What's the usual?' Kate enquired, as Spike left.

Grig laughed. 'Any Territorian would know. It's a few stubbies—beer, that is, or whatever your tipple happens to be.'

Kate wasn't really listening to him, she was immersed in her own thoughts. Why, she mused, would the coxswain seem to go to such trouble to let her know that naval marriages weren't easy, when she'd only just met him? Perhaps his wife would shed some light on that, she thought. She jolted back to her senses when Grig squeezed his six-foot-plus frame into the seat beside her and she found herself trapped.

'Cramped quarters have their advantages,' he observed, as his leg brushed hers. He laughed at her discomfort.

'Grig, behave yourself!' she said, in what she hoped sounded like a teasing voice.

'Why? I've got you where I want you now, and you know the reputation sailors have.' He leant over her to open the porthole and she sat transfixed, hypnotised like a rabbit by his deep azure eyes.

She knew he meant to kiss her and she had no way out. Rather than risk a commotion and appear foolish, she closed her eyes. Let him have his joke, she thought. I'll pretend it doesn't affect me, that should teach him. Nothing happened. She opened her eyes to see sparks of anger in his and the brilliant azure changed to steely grey.

'I had no intention of touching you,' he grated. 'God help Howard if you lie back and think of England every time he comes near you!'

'I wasn't thinking of England,' Kate protested, not knowing what else to say. 'Anyway, I'm Australian, not English.' She realised how foolish she sounded as soon as the words had left her lips. But she was incapable of retrieving them and explanations would only make matters worse.

'God help me! Ignorant as well as frozen!' Grig muttered under his breath and then started to laugh aloud.

'Don't you dare laugh at me!' Kate hissed, to avoid shouting.

'Why not? You're pretty funny at times.'

'You self-opinionated swine! I'm neither funny nor frozen. Yes, I did hear that last remark, and it's the last you'll make about me.' She slid round the table and stood up, ready to leave. But Grig's massive frame blocked the way, and as though he had done it many times before, he reached behind him and closed the curtain.

'Now, you said you weren't frozen. Let's find out, shall we?' he asked in a husky undertone.

'Grig, let me go!' Kate demanded. His arms encircled her and she found her head nestled under his chin.

'Only if you ask me nicely,' he whispered in her ear.

His hot breath sent shivers down her spine. He spun round, swinging her limp body with him, and rested on the edge of the table. Her face was now level with his and he tilted her chin with his finger, forcing her to look at him.

'Why in heaven's name Howard Monroe should have the misfortune to have tied himself up with a hazel-eyed witch like you I'll never know,' he whispered. His blue eyes darkened as he tilted her head and kissed her.

Kate's fists came up to pummel his chest. But the more she struggled, the tighter he held her. His lips were like ice—the sort of ice that burns, leaving an aching scar. She felt that the imprint of his lips would be there, on her own, forever. The ice turned to fire to consume her, leaving her weak and trembling.

His lips moved to the corner of her mouth, to the dimple that always appeared when she smiled. She was helpless. How did he know? He couldn't know. Even Howard didn't know. The thoughts raced through her bewildered brain. He'd found the one spot that made her melt. She was in his power. She wanted to be in his power, knowing still that she shouldn't want it. God, don't let him guess, was her last coherent thought as she lost herself in the wonder of him.

She sagged against him, fists relaxed, and helplessly began to caress his neck. Hypnotised, she stroked his face like a blind girl, tracing his features to implant them indelibly in her mind. Her nipples hardened, aching with the gentle friction of his body on hers. Unknowing, she pressed closer to stop the aching pleasure.

Suddenly Grig released her. She stood, disorientated and confused, the blood rushing to her cheeks. Breathing in uneven gasps, she tried to fathom the look in his stormy eyes. He was breathing hard and she noticed that his hands trembled as he lit two cigarettes.

'Well, well,' he said, smiling smugly. 'That certainly clears up the frozen image. And with a vengeance!'

He pushed her gently into a seat and handed her a cigarette. 'I'm not going to apologise for that. But I promise it won't happen again ... unless, that is, you want it too.'

'You're right, it won't happen again!' Kate cried, puffing distractedly on her cigarette. 'That wasn't fair to me or to Howie.'

'Oh? I suppose it wasn't fair at that. Still, I never was one to worry about being fair where a lady is concerned. Of course, if you change your

mind and want to throw fairness out the window,
I'll be only too happy to oblige.' His cynical,
bantering tone returned and he was once more in
complete control of himself. 'I know how strong-
willed you are, so I guess it's out of the question,'
he said, leaning over to stroke the place where the
dimple was.

'You're an ...' Kate was lost for words. 'I
wouldn't ask you to kiss me if you were the last
man on earth!'

'Stranger things have happened,' he told her
with a knowing look.

'Never, never. I'll never ask you, never!' Kate
almost screamed, her voice hoarse and husky with
defiance.

Her defiance brought a gleam to his eyes. 'Well
then, I'll just have to wait till you beg me,' he
mocked.

'Beg you! You've got about as much chance as
a snowball in hell!' Kate spat.

'For a lady, you have a colourful turn of
phrase, I've noticed,' Grig teased.

'And for a gentleman,' Kate threw back,
regaining her composure, 'you're an unmitigated
...' She couldn't think of a word bad enough
without swearing, and he burst out laughing.

'Come on, it wasn't that bad, and I'm sure
you've had advances made to you before. So I
can't see what all the fuss is about.'

She was speechless. He really thinks this is
something that happens to me all the time, she
thought. She started to get angry again. What
does he think I am? she asked herself.

She gathered her bag and hat together and

started out of the cabin, hoping to find her way to the quay and freedom.

'Where do you think you're going?' asked Grig.

'Back to the flat,' Kate told him, brushing him aside as she forced her way past him.

'Hang on. You'll never find your way alone.' He caught her by the arm and pulled her round to face him. He seemed perturbed at the tears that sparkled in her eyes, and she saw that he now knew he had overstepped her idea of good behaviour. He seemed puzzled and a little amused, but most of all regretful.

'Please don't run away,' he said. 'I'll take you back to the flat, if that's what you want.'

Kate felt a twinge of guilt. After all, she told herself, she hadn't exactly repulsed him. But I'm not going to let him see that I feel a bit guilty, she thought; let him feel like a heel, it'll do him good.

They didn't speak the whole way back in the car and Kate went straight to her room as soon as they arrived. She was still confused, guilty and angry, mostly at herself, but by remembering the taunts he had thrown her way, she was able to convince herself that she was angry with him and her contemplations fed the anger.

'I'll fix you, Grig Jacobsen,' she said aloud, her mind racing. 'You'll pay for that, and dearly!'

She pulled viciously at her hair with the brush, combing out the plait that he had seemed to like so much. I've got to pay him back, she told herself, but how? If I could make him fall in love with me, I'd have the whip hand then. Easier said than done, she mused. I wonder how a girl goes about making a man fall in love with her. But really, she continued to herself, I wouldn't need to make him fall in love with me, I'd only need to make him want to kiss me. Then I could laugh at him and his 'I'll wait till you beg!'

She blushed as the images of the time on the boat flashed through her mind. Arrogant, self-opinionated, chauvinistic ... She ran out of words to call him.

Calm down, she told herself. If you're going to get your own back, you'll have to hatch some sort of a plan. Now how does one go about getting a man to kiss one? she wondered. Come to think of it, she thought, I've never really wanted to do that before. The men I've kissed have all taken the initiative themselves and haven't needed any prompting.

If I'm to pull this stunt off, she mused, I'll have to get started, and I suppose there's no time like the present.

'Now let's see,' she said aloud, 'what would a tropical femme fatale wear?'

Opening her wardrobe doors, she surveyed the contents with a critical eye.

No, she mused, the evening dress slashed almost to the waist would be too obvious. The backless print? Maybe. I know, she thought, delighted with herself when the choice became apparent, I'll wear the red sarong.

She pulled it from its wrapping and examined it carefully. He picked it, she thought, so he should like it.

Feeling a bit uneasy at first, she watched her image in the mirror as she smoothed the bright scarlet material into place. She had to adjust it numerous times before she was happy that it would not come adrift, and she was forced to admit to herself that it did look stunning against the darkness of her hair that cascaded over her shoulders.

She went into the living room to see Grig sitting in one of the armchairs, with an ice-cold beer in his hands and a similar look in his eye. He eyed her up and down, and her resolve almost disintegrated as she felt him strip her mentally. But she looked back at him with disdain and without saying anything, headed for the kitchen.

Singing softly to herself to keep her courage up, Kate began to prepare a meal, and was soon lost in her enjoyment of the task. Cooking was an art she had learnt from her mother, and she enjoyed it immensely. So engrossed was she that she jumped when Grig's deep voice broke into her thoughts from just behind her.

'What do you think you're up to?' he asked sarcastically.

'If it's all the same to you,' she replied in kind, 'I'm making dinner.'

'Don't you know it's not ethical to use someone else's kitchen without permission?' he continued, ignoring her remark.

'Oh, isn't it?' Kate responded, with ice in her voice. 'Don't you know it's unethical to attempt to seduce a friend's fiancée?'

'Touché!' replied Grig with a chuckle, 'Can't blame a man for trying. Here, let me do those potatoes.' He moved closer to her and elbowed her out of the way to get at the sink.

'Got you where I want you!' thought Kate with

delight, and edged closer to him, rubbing her hip against his leg as if by accident.

Grig looked at her and she could see a question appear in his eyes, but she pretended she hadn't seen it.

She turned to reach for the condiments that were kept in a cupboard on the other side of the kitchen, and once more as if by accident, brushed past Grig. Her whole sarong-clad body touching his. She saw his eyes follow her as she bent to the stove, and realised that her sarong had slipped a little and that her breasts were almost bare.

Deliberately, she stood up and, facing him, began to adjust her clothes.

'Here, let me,' he said, reaching over to re-tie the sarong, his hands trailing across the tops of her breasts, sending cold shivers down her spine.

'Don't you know it's unethical to try to seduce your fiancé's friend?' he asked, his eyes never leaving hers as he brushed her hair gently back over her shoulders.

'I wasn't trying to seduce you, you self-opinionated lout!' Kate retorted angrily, her face scarlet.

'Oh, come on,' he replied laughing softly. 'I've been seduced by experts and an expert at it, you're not!'

'You—you——!' Kate was lost for words, knowing she had been caught out, and she shook his hands angrily from her shoulders, tears welling in her eyes.

'Look, if we're going to cohabit here peacefully till Howard gets back,' Grig said seriously. 'We'll have to put everything that's happened behind us and start again. I know I was out of line earlier, and I'm sorry.'

'Sorry!' Kate burst in, wiping the tears from her eyes with savage swipes of a tea towel. 'You wouldn't know the meaning of the word!'

'Sorry,' he said in a schoolboy sing-song. 'Regretful, repentant, grieved. I'm regretful that I caused you any embarrassment, repentant that my actions weren't welcomed, and grieved that you're already engaged to someone else. How's that for an apology?' he asked. 'That should soothe your wounded feelings and also help to keep your self-esteem. After all, you'd have been a bit miffed if I hadn't fancied you, wouldn't you?' he finished.

'You're impossible,' Kate replied, sniffling.

'I know, everyone tells me I am. Now go and wash your face and change out of that damned thing,' he said, pointing to the sarong. 'It will only give me ideas I shouldn't have. And if we're going to start over, you'll have to become Miss Modesty again.'

'What about dinner?' asked Kate, smiling weakly through the tears.

'I'll finish it. You go and get sorted out,' he replied, taking the fork from her hand and attacking the steak that had started to burn. 'I think I can save it.'

Half laughing, half crying that her scheme had come to nothing, Kate left the kitchen to follow his instruction.

Scrubbing her face reflectively in the bathroom, she resorted to her usual method of sorting out her feelings, having a conversation with herself.

'Perhaps you are making too much of that kiss on the boat. It isn't as if you're married to Howard yet.'

'True,' she answered herself.

'And he's right, you would have been a bit put out if he hadn't shown some interest.'

'Yes. But do you have to react like a schoolgirl when he's anywhere within fifty feet?' she asked herself sarcastically.

'I don't behave like a schoolgirl,' she told herself angrily, aware that her thinking had become personal and that it was a sign of her losing control. 'I didn't behave like this when Ken kissed me at the Christmas party or when that new doctor came on strong just before I left.'

'Well then, my girl, what's wrong with you now?'

'It must be the heat or that Howard wasn't here to meet me,' she answered herself.

'Rubbish, he's got to you.'

'He has not! I'm just not used to being alone all the time with a man.'

'That's a good excuse. You're just being plain juvenile, reacting this way to a normal man's reaction to being alone with an attractive woman.'

'I'm not that attractive. I'm not even good-looking,' Kate told herself, peering at herself in the mirror.

'Howard thinks so.'

'Yes, but Howard's different, he likes me for what I am, not how I look.'

'That's a funny way to put things. Howard doesn't just like you, he loves you. He told you so.'

'Yes, he did, didn't he? I'll have to hang on to that thought and stop behaving like some starstruck teenager.'

'If you must behave like a teenager, with a crush on Mr Wonderful, then Grig certainly fills the bill.'

'Rubbish, Howard's just as good-looking, and has as much sex appeal.'

'Suit yourself. But tell me, how come, when Grig tells you to jump, you jump? If Howard had told you to run away and wash your face there'd have been a blazing row over him telling you what to do.'

'Nonsense! Everything will fall back into place as soon as Howard gets back. I'm just a bit upset being here with a stranger, that's all.'

Satisfied that she had won the argument with herself, Kate changed into a dress and went out to help Grig with the dinner.

CHAPTER THREE

'Come on, sleepyhead!' Grig called through the bedroom door. 'Time to get up if you want to see the sights!'

'My God! What time is it?' Kate groaned, stretching and peering at the travelling clock she had put beside the bed. It was still dark and she had to switch on the light to see the time.

'You don't expect me to get up at this unholy hour?' she moaned, pulled the covers over her and buried her head under the pillow.

'It's five o'clock,' said Grig, bringing in a steaming mug. 'If you don't get up now, I'll pull the sheet off and douse you with cold water. That should do the trick,' he threatened.

'Slavedriver!' she muttered, sitting up to sleepily accept the proffered coffee from his outstretched hand.

'That's a nice way to be greeted in the morning!' he grinned. Kate assumed he was being sarcastic. But he added, 'Really makes a man's day.'

She looked at him and followed his eyes. Her nightdress had slipped, exposing a rather large expanse of flesh.

'Very nice indeed,' he grinned again, rubbing his hands.

'Get out. Go and find someone else to ogle,' said Kate, adjusting herself.

'Or you'll what?'

'I'll throw something at you,' she retorted, placing the coffee carefully on the floor.

'Now that wouldn't be ladylike,' he teased.

'Ladylike be blowed! Gentlemen don't stand ogling ladies in their bedrooms,' she threw back, half laughing. Trying to hide her embarrassment hadn't worked and she flamed scarlet right down to her now partially covered bust.

'Never claimed to be a gentleman,' said Grig, gazing with unabashed admiration at her cleavage. He ducked smartly as a pillow sailed past his ear.

'I know when I'm not wanted. But it's still time for you to get up,' he threw over his shoulder as he left, slamming the door.

Kate jumped out of bed and padded into the bathroom. The lacy confection that was her night attire slipped easily over her head. She stood in front of the mirror, taking in her image critically.

Her breasts weren't bad really. A bit full perhaps for her slight figure, she thought. But her legs, muscled and shaped well, from dancing, were good. Maybe she could work on her tan today. Grig didn't appear to be a leg man, she mused, so she shouldn't have too many problems with him if she wore shorts.

She twisted her hair up on top of her head and pinned it before climbing into the shower. Humming to herself as she lathered her body, she thought of Howard. Won't it be great to see him again and to have him kiss me? She tried to remember what his kisses were like, but found she could only remember Grig's lips. God damn him, that episode on the boat was going to haunt her till she could see Howard again.

Damn him, damn him! It was only because it had been so long since she had seen Howard, and Grig was right here that he was affecting her like this. Hold on to thoughts of Howie, she told herself savagely, and the animal magnetism of Mr High and Mighty Grig Jacobsen will pale into insignificance, like that. She clicked her fingers.

Laughing to herself, at her juvenile-seeming antics, she climbed out of the shower and dried herself carefully, still not able, for all her good intentions, to put the memory of Grig's kiss from her mind. With a will of its own, her mind lingered on the time on the boat, and her stomach contracted with the butterflies that had weakened her so much at the time.

I don't really like him *that* much, she mused. That's not true, her heart said. He's really quite sweet at times. No, you couldn't call him sweet, more like intoxicating, but she wasn't interested in an intoxicating man. Stop lying, she told herself. If you weren't so happy with Howard, you'd jump at the chance.

To hell with him! He's only showing me round till Howard gets back, no need to take too much trouble with how I look, Kate thought as she pulled on a pair of brief denim shorts and adjusted a matching waistcoat-like top. She had always felt comfortable in it, and the high cut-out sleeveless design allowed her to go braless. That had to be a plus in the Darwin heat.

She peered at her face in the glass and decided on a minimum of make-up. Lipstick and a touch of eyeliner would do. Then slipping her feet into leather thongs, she dug out her cartwheel sunhat and was ready.

As she threw her hat and bag on to a chair in the lounge, the smell of frying bacon assaulted her nostrils, making her mouth water in hungry anticipation.

'Looks good,' she said, wandering into the kitchen to catch Grig in the act of shovelling bacon and eggs on to plates.

'So do you,' he replied, eyeing her up and down. 'I hope you've got plenty of suntan lotion or you'll get burnt with all that virgin skin exposed. Without it you'll stay that colour,' he teased, noticing her blush. 'Here, sit down and stoke up for the day. It could be a while before we eat again.'

She sat opposite him and, regardless of his bantering, tucked in with a will.

'Nice to see a woman who doesn't pick at her food,' he said, helping himself to more coffee and pouring her another.

'I can't stand girls who are always dieting!'

'I guess I'm lucky,' Kate commented. 'I've never had any problems with my weight. I can eat anything.'

'Good,' said Grig, changing the subject, leaving her to wonder why her weight or lack of it should be of concern to him.

'I hope you're planning on taking a swimsuit. I thought we'd head for Berry Springs first for a swim before the crowd gets there. And if we want to miss them, we'd better get going.' He stacked the dishes in the sink and ran the hot water over them.

'I'll wash those,' Kate offered.

'Not now. They can wait till later. Get your gear,' he ordered. 'We're off.'

Kate dashed hurriedly to her room to find a swimsuit, then picking up her bag and hat looked up to find Grig drumming impatiently on the door.

'I'm ready,' she said.

'About time too. I never met a woman yet who didn't take forever to get organised. And some of them never could.'

'You talk as if you were an expert on the subject. You must have had a lot to get that experienced,' Kate said quietly to his towering back, sticking out her tongue as she did. She was surprised when he replied. She had thought she'd spoken softly enough for him not to hear.

'How come you're so interested in my private life all of a sudden?' he asked, glancing back over his shoulder catching her with her tongue out. 'Cheeky as well as curious,' he added, smiling to himself. 'I'll have to watch myself, won't I?'

Kate followed him down the stairs, subdued. I've put my foot in it again, she thought. He'll keep ribbing me all day now. Maybe, if I just keep my mouth shut and answer when I'm spoken to, I'll be able to stay out of trouble. Determining to play safe with this man she couldn't fathom and whose every word and action seemed to be new, exciting and unique, Kate followed him in silence.

'We'll take Howard's car, I think. Less chance of sunstroke,' said Grig, passing the now familiar and dear little red car and escorting her to the one he had pointed out previously as Howard's.

Within minutes, they were spinning through the outskirts of Darwin, past the airport and the notorious Casey's Corner. Past the experimental farm and the Air Force radio station and on down the track, with the sun just bursting over the horizon flooding the gum trees with its rosy light. It was still cool, at least for the Territory, but the cloudless skies gave notice of a typical top end scorcher.

Kate gazed silently at the passing scenery, hoping with a typical southerner's hope to see some wildlife. Somehow she had expected to see dingoes, kangaroos and perhaps even a tribal aborigine or two on walkabout. But all she saw was an old goanna and the never-ending eucalypts.

Grig seemed to have read her mind, as he commented, 'Nothing much to see on the track. The wildlife has enough sense to keep well away from the road and you have to get off it to see anything much. And if you want to see wild natives, as so many visitors do, you'd need to go well inland. There aren't many left now that haven't had some contact with the white man.'

Kate didn't comment and they turned off the main road into a secondary one with a sign marked Berry Springs, in silence, only broken by the hum of the tyres on bitumen.

She was surprised to see that the popular picnic spot was a well kept, grassed parkland with barbecues dotted around among the trees. She found the toilet and changing rooms spotless and well cared for as she changed into a strapless, figure-hugging pink and black one-piece suit.

She hurried out to find Grig already dressed for the water in a brief suit that left very little to the imagination and allowed her to admire his massive physique. Part of her wanted to pluck out the eyes that she couldn't control as they roved over his six-foot frame.

Hussy, she called herself, as she took in the superb shoulders which sloped to a well muscled chest, matted with the same golden hair that adorned his head. Her fingers ached to touch it and she flexed them to stop them tingling. She continued her scrutiny through her sunglasses, hoping Grig wouldn't become aware of it.

She sat on the concrete wall that surrounded part of the natural pool, dangling her feet in the water and watching him as he prepared to dive in. There wasn't an ounce of spare flesh on his almost too-slim waist and hips that tapered to the legs that had so affected her the first time they had met.

Trying to take her mind off the body that could, against her will, turn her to jelly, she removed her glasses and looked around with interest.

The main pool was quite large and surrounded by massive native trees, one of which leaned over the middle of the pool and had, by the attachment of a rope and tyre, been turned into a makeshift swing. The whole scene made an oasis of peace and coolness in the burning Territory sun. A creek ran into the pool at the top, exiting near where she was sitting, trickling musically over large river rocks forming smaller, shallower pools that were safe for little children.

She wished she had brought her camera, but that had been forgotten in the rush to get out. She determined to return here with Howard in the hope that his presence would erase the memory of Grig from this romantic and lovely spot, and that with Howard in the photographs she would only think of him when she recalled it.

So wrapped in the confusion of her own thoughts was she that she didn't see Grig paddle silently up to her until he had grabbed her by the ankles and pulled her in.

'Beast!' she spluttered, surfacing breathless and laughing.

'Couldn't let you sit there all day communing with nature. There's more to see.' He swam off, leaving her to follow.

Kate swam after him across the pool to the creek where they were forced, by the shallowness of the water, to wade knee-deep upstream against the current, through a tangle of overhanging branches that formed a sort of tunnel. They emerged at the end into another clearing and a pool somewhat smaller than the main one, but breathtaking in its morning beauty.

Kate gasped in delight at the sight that caught her gaze. A waterfall, swift-flowing but small enough to sit under, was creating the noise that had puzzled her for the past few minutes. It was formed by the creek flowing over a rocky ledge at the upper end of the pool and cascaded, boiling, into the water below.

'Come on!' Grig called, already sitting beneath the spray. 'It's better than a massage!'

Kate joined him and allowed the thundering

torrent to pound on her back, almost knocking her over with the force of it. She had never felt so invigorated, and she turned kneeling under the spray to let it thunder on to her head and shoulders. The force was so great that she was forced to hold her swimsuit up. Grig saw her struggles and pulled her down into the calmer waters of the pool.

'I'd better get you out of here before you start showing yourself off again. I've never met a woman with such an overwhelming urge to bare all,' he said, leading her by the hand out of the water and up a steep flight of steps that cut through the heavy bush and brought them back to the park.

They strolled in companionable silence to the place where they had left their clothes and sprawled on the towels to enjoy the morning sun.

'Better put some suntan lotion on,' said Grig, lighting a cigarette and handing her one.

Kate's eyebrows raised as she took it without comment, surprised that he had remembered, and knew without being told that she felt like one. She rummaged in her bag to find the lotion and her sunglasses and, after finishing her cigarette, began to smooth on the cream. She applied it carefully to her legs, arms, neck and throat, feeling his eyes on her. She turned in time to catch him and felt pleased with herself somehow when he appeared abashed. He recovered quickly by asking, 'Want me to do your back?'

'Mm, yes,' Kate purred. Score one for me, she thought, turning on to her stomach.

He poured the lotion between her shoulder-blades and started to massage it into her skin. His hands were strong but gentle and she felt the blood pulse in her veins at his touch. He kneaded the muscles at the base of her neck and she moaned with pleasure.

He pushed the wet hair off her neck and rubbed it with his thumbs, sending waves of electricity through her entire being. As his kneading hands moved down her spine, Kate felt her nipples harden and her body betray her, revelling in the eroticism of his touch.

She knew she should move or stop him, but she was powerless. His hands were hypnotic and she lay there, if he had only known, completely at his mercy, her mind saying stop, but her body worshipping his touch, wanting it never to end.

'Hedonistic little beast, aren't you?' he remarked, planting a light kiss on the back of her neck. 'Your turn.'

Kate rolled over, hoping he wouldn't notice the state she was in. But he had already turned over, waiting for her to oil his back. She knelt beside him, poured on the lotion and, with her practised nurse's hands, began to massage it in.

Grig made no bones about the pleasure it gave him, moaning with delight at the movement of her hands. In an attempt to overcome the sensations she felt herself, Kate increased the pressure, hoping it would become intolerable and he would ask her to stop.

'That's lovely,' he groaned. 'A bit to the left, you've missed a spot.'

'How would you know?' she asked. 'You can't see.'

'No, but I can feel, and you've missed that bit. That's better,' he said, as she massaged where he had indicated.

Kate continued stroking and massaging long after she had covered his back with the lotion, even adding more just so she could still touch him, castigating herself the whole time for her inability to stop.

'You'd better stop that now, woman,' Grig moaned through clenched teeth, 'or I won't be responsible for my actions!'

'Don't tell me that bothers you,' Kate teased aloud, but shaking inwardly, pleased, once more against her will, that he had had to ask her to stop. Score two to me, she thought.

'That bothers me as long as it's a female doing it,' he rumbled into the grass, shattering the fragile illusion that her hands were the cause of his obvious enjoyment.

'Pity any girl who gets tied up with you. She'll spend most of her time rubbing your back then,' Kate retorted, in an effort to make a joke of it.

'That's not all she'll be rubbing,' he bantered, not to be outdone. He looked up to catch her blushing and his great laugh boomed out, filling the silent air and reverberating through the empty park. Kate's clear musical laughter joined his and their voices merged to startle the sleepy kookaburras into their own wild cacophony of mirth.

'Enough of this pandering to the flesh! Lots more places to see. Get your gear on, I want to go and watch the birds—feathered variety, that is,' he added, springing to his feet and marching off in the direction of the car, leaving Kate to collect their towels and find her own way to the changing shed.

By the time she reached the car, dressed once more in her shorts, about a dozen other cars had arrived, spilling people and picnic gear out and ruining the peaceful atmosphere with the noise of humanity.

'The place will be a madhouse soon,' said Grig, watching the scene with obvious distaste. 'Best we get out now.'

Kate noticed that he was still in his swimsuit and had only pulled his tee-shirt on to cover his bare chest.

'Where are we going now?' she asked, wondering how he could drive barefoot.

'You've heard of Humpty Doo, where they tried to grow rice a few years ago?' he asked. 'Well, that's become a sort of huge lagoon now and is full of thousands of birds. If we're lucky, we might even see some brolgas.'

'They're the birds in the aboriginal legends, aren't they?' Kate interrupted.

'That's right—they dance. Anyway, after that I thought we could have lunch at the Humpty Doo pub. Then we should have enough time to go home and change. Sheila and Spike are expecting us for dinner.'

They spent a number of hours watching the birds, and Kate found herself becoming as fascinated with them as Grig was. The brolgas were out and danced gracefully as any ballerinas just for them. Kate watched in wonder and felt she knew just what the female brolga was feeling as she dipped and swayed round the male, her every movement saying 'I love you' so clearly that Kate felt like an intruder.

A city girl, she had only ever seen animals up close at the zoo, and had never felt the need to commune with nature before. This was a new experience to her, so new and thrilling in its uniqueness that it took her breath away and she was moved almost to tears.

With great ease, Grig pointed out lizards and small marsupials and took her to see the buffaloes that came to the fence in their docile, magnificent splendour. The calves, a soft, velvety-pink colour, compared to the tough, greyish-brown hide of their parents. She wondered at the ability of nature to endow her creatures with the camouflage they needed to survive, while leaving her most impressive achievement, man, naked and vulnerable to the elements with only his brainpower to survive.

She was stunned and overjoyed at this new aspect of life and said very little as they roamed around the area, and her silence made Grig ask if she was feeling all right when they sat down for lunch at the Humpty Doo pub.

The hotel was small and one-storied, with a verandah round two sides. It was far from the types of places she was used to and the meals, served across the bar, could hardly be called Cordon Bleu, but it had atmosphere like none she had ever encountered before and she felt comfortable and at ease.

'I've never seen anything like it,' she told him, over their steak sandwiches.

'You should see Katherine Gorge,' he replied. 'It should be classified, in my opinion, as one of the wonders of the world.'

'Is it far?' she asked.

'Too far for me to take you,' he answered. 'Maybe Howard will be able to take you when he gets back. You really need to go down for a couple of days to see the whole place properly.'

At the mention of Howard, Kate came back to earth with a thud. He had been far from her thoughts all day and she felt disloyal somehow, that she had been shown something that affected her so profoundly, by another man. An experience as beautiful as this should have been shared with the man she planned to spend the rest of her life with.

This was one more case of Grig shaking up her well-established attitudes on life. She knew that Howard wouldn't have been interested and, up till now, she would have accepted his judgment that a trip like this would be a waste of a day that could be spent much more leisurely. For, far from being idle, they had walked for miles, leaving the car and tramping through the bush to see the sights that had so enraptured her.

The thought crossed her mind that if she married Howard, days like these would be a thing of the past instead of adventures she could look forward to. For she had decided early in their nature walk that she must do more of this sort of thing in other places. There was so much she had never seen. And much, she knew, she should have seen, very close to her home in Sydney.

Looking up, she saw Grig surveying her closely with a quizzical look in his eyes. She hadn't been aware that her thoughts were readable. But then, she pondered, it seems that G. Jacobsen Esquire has the unfortunate knack of reading me like a book.

'What are the plans for dinner?' she asked, to take her mind on to more mundane matters.

'We're due at a barbecue at Spike and Sheila's, so I suppose we'd better think about heading home to change.' To Kate's ears he seemed to have put an emphasis on the 'home', but she refused to rise to the bait, if indeed it was, and just nodded agreement.

They drove home in companionable silence, Kate seeing things in the bush that would have escaped her before today. Somehow in their nature walk Grig had managed, without seeming to, to install an awareness that she had not had before.

At the flat, Kate showered and changed into a long slim jersey patio dress. High at the front and almost backless, its soft lavender folds clung in all the right places. She piled her hair on top of her head and caught it with two matching combs, her colouring and hairstyle giving her an almost Spanish look.

She was surprised to see Grig in slacks and shirt, definately more urbane than his usual shorts and tee-shirt.

'What's the occasion?' she asked.

'None. I just felt like being civilised for a change,' he growled. Kate saw that he was somewhat embarrassed.

'Why don't you go out on the balcony,' she suggested, 'while I get my camera. I must have a photo of you looking civilised.'

'I wouldn't push my luck if I were you,' he snarled, 'or I'll get out of these and into my sarong.'

'You wouldn't go visiting in that, would you?'

'Why not? They've seen me in it before. Come to think of it, they'll probably think I'm a bit strange appearing in this get-up,' he said, pulling angrily at the neck of his shirt.

'Well, I think you look very handsome.' Kate could have bitten her tongue off as soon as the words left her mouth. Grig's sardonic grin appeared for the first time for hours and his eyes gleamed with mischief.

'Did you say handsome? Compliments now! What have I done to deserve this?'

His tone was facetious and Kate was hard pressed not to laugh. 'Now you mention it,' she said, 'it's more like human than handsome.'

'Just because you look like a million dollars, it doesn't mean you can get away with that! I warned you about being cheeky, and that constitutes cheek in any language.' He moved towards her threateningly and she backed away, not sure whether he was serious or not. She realised he had every intention of carrying out his earlier threat when he caught her by the arm and pulled her across his knee.

'Don't, Grig!' she wailed, half-laughing. 'You'll mess up my dress!'

'Do you want to take it off first, then?' he asked, patting her wriggling, round bottom lovingly. She squirmed, trying to escape, still unsure of his intentions.

'You're incorrigible,' she told him, pulling out of his not too tight grasp and managing to rise to her feet.

'I'll let you off this time,' he grinned. 'But only because you're dressed to go out. Anyway, Spike and Sheila would be a bit upset if you couldn't sit down. Don't let it happen again.'

Damn, damn! Kate thought, I never know when he's serious. She smoothed down her dress and patted her hair, making sure it was in place.

'Don't worry, you still look beautiful.'

Kate appraised him through her lashes, to determine if he were teasing, and was startled to see that he was serious. He noticed her watching him and turned away quickly. 'Come on, enough primping. It's time we left,' he said, and led her to the door.

Sheila and Spike lived in one of the new cyclone-proof houses that had been built since Cyclone Tracy had devastated Darwin a few Christmases before. It was a concrete split-level, white with green trim, identical to most of the other houses in the street except for the trimmings, which were different for each.

The carport was situated beneath the upper level and served as an outdoor living area when the car was removed. The Joneses had spent a great deal of time and effort to make the area around the carport attractive, since most of their entertaining took place there. An attractive creeper grew profusely up a trellis, acting as a screen to enclose the side, and banana trees and tapioca palms at the back gave the impression of a tropical garden. Outdoor furniture had been placed near the barbecue and pot plants hung from baskets from the overhead beams. Kate was reminded of pictures of island paradises and she was tempted to tell Grig that his sarong would have been more suitable after all.

'Beer, Kate?' asked Spike, handing one to Grig and motioning them to the seats.

'Not at the moment, thanks. It's a bit early for me. I'll have a soft drink if you have one.'

'You can tell she's a newcomer,' taunted Grig. 'Give her another couple of weeks and she'll be drinking beer with the rest of us!'

'The soft drinks are in the kitchen fridge,' said Spike. 'I'll just get one.'

'I'll go,' Kate told him, rising and following the soft singing voice that she assumed was Sheila's.

As she entered the kitchen, she heard Grig tell Spike, 'She probably wants to gossip with Sheila about the Navy and Darwin.' She smiled to herself. She had been thinking that she'd leave the men to gossip about the Navy and Darwin, while she got to know her hostess.

Sheila Jones was busily preparing salads in the large, airy kitchen and welcomed Kate with a bright smile. She was an attractive woman in her late thirties who exuded an air of competence and contentment. She was dressed for the heat in a strapless floor-length patio dress, and it was evident that she wore no bras and that she needed none. Her movements were those of a person who knew exactly what she was doing and was happy doing it.

'How are you enjoying Darwin?' she asked, deftly chopping onions to add to the salad she was making.

'Tha heat's a bit hard to take. But I expect I'll get used to it,' answered Kate, picking up a knife and starting to shred the already washed lettuce.

'Takes a while, I know. Trouble is once you're used to it, it's hard to take the cold when you go back south,' said Sheila, putting the finished salad into the fridge and taking out a bottle of lemonade. 'Let's have a drink. Spike never thinks to ask the ladies if they'll have one. He's so used to me not drinking much that he forgets.'

'Oh! He asked me, but I didn't feel like a beer,' Kate replied.

'That's typical. The men up here think everyone drinks beer. Still, you should be honoured he asked you. He must be trying to impress,' said Sheila with an infectious laugh, and Kate found herself laughing too.

Sheila handed her a tall glass of wine and lemonade with ice cubes and they sat at the table sipping it.

'I suppose I'm really not entitled to say this under the circumstances,' Sheila began hesitantly.

'Say what?' asked Kate.

'Well—I don't like interfering, but it's so obvious that someone's going to say it, so it's better, I think, if it comes from someone who wishes you no harm.'

'What are you trying to tell me?'

'Oh, hell! I've done it now!' groaned Sheila.

'Please tell me,' burst in Kate, as Sheila hesitated.

'It's about Grig. People are talking about you two.'

'But I've only been here two days!'

'That's enough up here. Word gets around very quickly in an isolated place like Darwin.'

'But why?' Kate was genuinely perplexed.

'Well, Grig is a pretty popular guy. He's greatly in demand and usually socialises quite freely when he's here. But he's cancelled a couple of parties because you're here and refused to take you when they asked, so the girls are pretty upset,' Sheila explained.

'But that's not my fault. I didn't know.'

'I know that, but they don't.'

'Well, you can let them know they've nothing to fear from me. I'm already engaged.'

'Yes, I'd heard,' Sheila said quietly. 'Look, Kate, if anything goes wrong with you and Howard and you need someone to talk to, I'll listen. Everyone needs a friend in a strange place. So if things go a bit haywire . . .' she broke off.

'What could possibly go wrong?' Kate asked anxiously.

'You never can tell,' said Sheila. 'Just remember what I said and we'll leave it at that.'

Kate was surprised at Sheila's words, but decided it probably was best to leave things as they were. Everything would come right as soon as Howard returned and any gossip about her and Grig would stop. Remembering Spike's comments from earlier about Naval marriages, she decided to ask his wife what he had meant.

'Sheila, can I ask you something rather personal?'

'As long as it isn't for a loan of Spike,' she quipped, 'you can ask me anything you like.'

'Well, it is about Spike in a way.'

'The old devil! He told me he thought you were a pretty smashing-looking bird, but he didn't tell me he'd made a conquest,' Sheila laughed, letting Kate know that she was joking.

'Actually, it's about something he said yesterday.'

'He's always saying something and leaving people to wonder what he meant.'

'He said that you and he had a Naval marriage that had survived, and I got the impression he was trying to warn me about something.'

'Mm . . . That's one of his hobbyhorses, I'm afraid,' Sheila said seriously. 'You see, the percentage of divorces in Navy families is very high and it takes a lot of work and effort to make them work.'

'Oh!' said Kate, bewildered. The thought that marriage to a sailor should be any different from anyone else had never entered her head.

'Sailors and their wives have more problems than most. Mainly it's the amount of time the men are away.'

Sheila took a long sip of her drink before continuing. 'It's very hard for a young woman to cope with all the problems of raising a family when her husband is away for two years out of three. It's hard on the kids too. Sometimes they're born while their fathers are away and when he does get back he's a stranger.'

'I hadn't thought of those sort of problems,' Kate said pensively.

'Spike and I went through some pretty tough times in the beginning. But I must admit he'd warned me how hard it would be. That's something a lot of the sailors don't tell their wives before they're married, and the poor girls get an awful shock.'

'How did you cope?'

'Well, in the beginning, I was determined to be as close to Spike as possible, and I moved to the different bases where his ships would berth, so that I'd see him whenever they came in for any reason. It's called living in the ship's home port. Eventually, we realised that it wasn't the best solution for us, and I moved to his home town so that I could have his family near to help me raise the children.'

'Didn't that mean you didn't see as much of him as you would have?' Kate queried.

'Yes, it did, and I sometimes felt that if I'd been stronger I could have coped with all the moving. But we'd made our decision and it was the best for us in the long run.'

'Why did Spike feel he had to tell me about it?' Kate asked, still a little confused.

'He feels that girls thinking about marrying Navy guys should be told what they're in for— really told, I mean. Told about the months of loneliness and about making a life for themselves while their husbands are away that they have to give up when he gets back. Told about how hard it is to bring up a family by themselves. Told about coping with emergencies on their own.'

'But surely love comes into all this, doesn't it?' Kate broke in.

'Sure. But it has to be a very special type of love.'

'But, Sheila, if you love someone, you love him. How can you have a special kind of love?'

'I can't explain it really. We've seen couples who were so in love it was hard to imagine them apart, yet they didn't survive. Over the years, I've come to the conclusion that it's the sort of love where he's your best friend, you lover, your brother . . . I don't know. I only know that when Spike's away it feels as if half of me's missing and no one can be that other half.'

'How do you know if you have that?'

'I can't speak for anyone else, but for me it was just that I loved him and hated him all at the same time. If we had a barney, I hated him, but I didn't want him to leave, and when he did leave there was something missing till he got back. What a subject to be talking about!' Sheila exclaimed suddenly. 'We're supposed to be enjoying ourselves, not getting into things like this. Let's go and have a drink with the fellows while Spike throws the steaks on the fire.' She rose and followed by Kate took her drink to the carport.

Kate tried to put Sheila's words out of her mind, but they kept coming back to worry her. I've never felt like that about Howard, she thought. In fact, sometimes I didn't think about him for days, and then a letter would come and he'd be on my mind for a while. Nonsense, she told herself, that just goes to prove I'll be able to cope when he's away. Well, if that's true, why are you behaving like you have been with Grig?

'Something on your mind?' asked Grig, as they drove back to the flat. 'You've been somewhere else all evening.'

'Just tired, I think,' Kate answered, feeling guilty about lying to him, but unable to tell him what had been bothering her.

'Looks as though we might get a storm tonight,' Grig's voice broke into her thoughts as they pulled into the parking area at the flats. 'I'd better put the cover over my car.' He handed her the flat keys. 'Let yourself in, I'll be a couple of minutes yet. Oh, by the way, Howard's car is in that garage there,' he pointed to one of the garages under the flats. 'He's left the keys for you so you can use it while he's away.'

Kate nodded absently and taking the flat keys hurried upstairs, anxious to get to bed before he finished covering his car. She had a great deal to ponder over and she knew that if he wanted to he would be able to make her tell him what had been bothering her, and she wasn't prepared to do that. Not yet.

CHAPTER FOUR

GREAT jagged streaks of lightning, lighting up the room like a spotlight, dragged Kate from a dreamless sleep to horrified reality. In terror she leapt from the bed, almost tearing the curtains from their tracks as she jerked them closed.

The thunder drove her back to the bed and she huddled in the middle, pulling the sheets over her head, in a vain effort to block the sounds from her ears.

But it didn't work. Nothing worked at times like these. Shaking uncontrollably, she scurried, between peals, to the bathroom. She had to find them. She'd put them in, she knew she had. God! Don't let me have forgotten them, she cried in anguish.

My pills, she moaned to herself, my pills. Oh, dear God, let me find them! The sedatives were the only things that helped Kate in thunderstorms and she scrabbled through her toilet bag in search of them.

The uncontrollable shaking of her hands made her drop the precious bag, and she fell to her knees, rummaging amongst the scattered toilet items to find the elusive pill bottle.

Every clap of thunder sent shock-waves through her body, making her scatter the contents far and wide over the bathroom floor. They're not here, she wailed. What am I going to do? They're not here! Finally, in despair, she cowered in the corner against the shower, arms crossed and hugging her own shoulders, numbly swaying to and fro in a paroxysm of fear.

'My God, woman, don't you realise what time it is?' Grig's angry voice broke through to her frozen senses. 'What in hell's name is going on?' he asked, rubbing his hands through his hair and gazing in amazement at the debris-littered floor.

Kate's rasping sobs brought his sleepy brain to full alert and he covered the floor in a single stride, sweeping her up into iron-strong arms and carrying her easily to the living room.

She threw her arms convulsively round his neck, clinging as though her life depended on it and burrowing deeper into the curve of his shoulder every time the thunder roared.

'You're terrified,' his soft voice murmured in her ear, soft enough for it to have been to himself. 'Don't be—it's only thunder.'

'I can't help it,' Kate whispered brokenly. 'Oh God, there it is again!' She clung to him quivering in panic.

Grig sat down, cradling her in his lap like a frightened child. He stroked her hair, murmuring nonsense words, his voice soothing and gentle. 'It's all right, darling, it's O.K. I won't let it hurt you. There, there, calm down.' Over and over, like a litany.

Gradually her fear abated and her trembling hands eased their vicelike grip on his neck.

'Now, honey,' he rumbled, deep in his throat, reminding Kate of a great bear, 'tell old Grig all about it.'

Her voice still shook and she gulped to clear her throat. It took a moment before she could bring herself to speak without shaking. 'I was lost in a thunderstorm when I was small.' Her voice was small and weak, almost childlike as she relived the horror of the memory. 'I was lost and scared, and I've been terrified of storms ever since.'

'O.K., that I can understand,' he said in a strong, calm tone that jerked Kate back to the present. 'Now, what was all that nonsense in the bathroom?'

She smiled weakly. She was shy, somehow, of admitting to this man that she needed pills to cope with something he obviously took in his giant stride. 'I was trying to find my sedatives,' she whispered, in her little-girl voice. 'I have some just for times like this.'

'You'll never get over it if you have to resort to that sort of thing,' he said severely. 'Doesn't anything else work?'

The words stuck in her throat, but she managed to get them out, strangling on the admission. 'I'm usually not too bad if someone stays with me.'

With shaking hands, she extricated herself from his lap. Removing his encircling arms that still held her tight, she rose to her feet. Eyes wide with terror, she froze as another thunderclap reverberated through the room. Shaking and swaying, she grabbed for support that wasn't there.

Grig caught her before she could fall, pulling her firmly against him, comforting her with his very presence.

'This storm is liable to last for another couple of hours, little one,' he breathed into her hair. 'So, what am I going to do with you?'

The fear was real, almost tangible, and she pleaded, desperation driving all pride from her mind, 'Don't leave me. Please don't leave me!'

'I won't leave you, honey—it's all right, I won't leave you.' His voice was a soothing singsong. Over and over he repeated his words, his hands stroking and gentling her like a frightened colt.

'Do you think you could sleep if I stayed with you till you dropped off?' he asked, obviously concerned.

'I don't know,' she whispered. 'I've never been in a storm as loud as this before.'

He tipped her head up to look directly into her face, then guiding her by the shoulders to her bedroom he said, 'Let's try it, shall we?'

The storm seemed to lull, and Kate's jangled nerves quietened. She blushed, noticing for the first time since the lightning had wakened her that she was clad only in the pretty but flimsy nightie she had chosen earlier for coolness. The sight of Grig in only his pyjama bottoms added to her confusion and embarrassment, but he seemed unmoved as he tucked her into bed.

He sat on the edge of the bed and stroked her hand. 'Feeling better?' he asked, patting her hand in a rhythmical, calming way.

Kate's eyes drooped sleepily. 'Mn ... yes, thanks,' she mumbled.

He was almost to the door, padding softly on bare feet. The thunder roared as if Thor himself were just outside the window, and Kate's eyes snapped open. 'Grig, please don't leave me!' Her voice was a pitiful wail.

In an instant, he was beside her, holding her. She grasped for his neck, pulling him sprawling down beside her. 'Hold me,' she begged. 'Please hold me—I'm so scared!'

The sheets seemed to disappear as he took her completely in his massive, safe arms, moulding her against his body and stroking her back and neck. His soothing words and warm closeness combined to blot out the storm, and a calm spread through her veins—a calm she had never felt before. The vague feeling that she shouldn't be in his arms died almost before it was born. The 'rightness' of the moment overwhelmed her and she sighed.

The soft murmuring of Grig's words was music to her panicstricken ears, soft, gentle, soul-easing melodies that lulled her fears and made her want to stay for ever.

Her hands, that had been locked around his neck, moved of their own accord to stroke his hair, and her body pressed unbidden closer to his. Closer to the comfort and fear-defying warmth that enclosed her like a cocoon.

'Darling, darling,' she heard him say, 'it's all right—I won't let anything hurt you. Not even one strand of this beautiful hair.' His words were meaningless. Only the soothing rhythm of them had meaning. 'Hush, hush, baby, I'm here. Everything will be fine, I promise. I won't leave you, I won't leave you.'

'Grig, I'm sorry,' she moaned. 'I shouldn't be such a baby. But I'm so glad you're here.'

The murmuring melodies ceased as he gently untangled her fingers from his hair and rose on one elbow to search her face. Kate felt bereft. An overwhelming sense of loss caused tears to spill uncalled from her already tear-stained eyes. He wiped them gently away with his finger, a look of almost amusement, but not quite laughter, in his eyes, a look that said everything and nothing. A desperate desire to know what it meant filled her, but instinct stopped her from asking.

He smiled down at her, chasing the tears across her cheek with his finger. The silence was intense and Kate was loath to break it, but words seemed called for and she spoke without thinking. 'Thank you, Grig. I don't know what I'd have done if you hadn't been here.'

His eyes changed from azure-blue to hard, steely grey and his expression from amusement to anger. Her heart lurched. She reached out tentatively to touch him, but he brushed her hand away. 'I forgot, didn't I?' he asked savagely. 'You still think I'm some sort of Top End Casanova, unfit to touch your lily-white body. Still, I came in handy for something, didn't I?'

'Oh, Grig, I didn't . . .'

'You didn't what?' he spat, sitting up. 'Didn't really want me to hold you? It was an act, wasn't it? And I fell for it hook, line and sinker.'

'An act? What do you mean?,' Kate cried, bewildered. 'It wasn't an act!'

He looked at her with contempt. 'Oh no? Wasn't this your way of getting revenge for our little scene on the boat? God knows, you tried hard enough to turn me on last night, but I wasn't half asleep then. You should try out for T.V.—you're quite an actress!'

'But, Grig . . .' she broke in.

'Don't bother adding insult to injury,' he snarled. 'You've proved you point. You didn't have to beg. Now let's leave it at that. I've got a boat to get out tomorrow and I need all the sleep I can get, so I'll just leave you to gloat over your victory.'

Leaning over her so that she cowered away from the anger in his face, he held her chin in a grip of iron and grated, 'If I weren't a gentleman of sorts, I'd knock your pretty little head off!'

Tears spilled unheeded from Kate's eyes. She was speechless, unable and unwilling, now, to explain. Mute, when she needed to tell him that revenge had never entered her head. Wordless, when her soul cried out for him to hold her again and keep her safe from the storm that still raged outside.

Three mighty roars of Thor's hammer sounded, one after the other, like some giant trying to demolish the building. Kate stared at him, trying to tell him with fear-filled eyes of the horror that gripped her.

Turning at the door, he took in her frightened state. 'I told you you'd proved your point. No need to do an encore,' he growled.

Kate cowered in the middle of the bed, shaking, her hands over her ears. 'Please, please, don't leave me alone,' she begged. 'Please, Grig, I'll do anything, if you don't leave me alone!'

Round-eyed, silently pleading, she watched him move slowly towards her in the glow of the bedside lamp. Breathless, she watched as he took her by the shoulder and stared deep into her face, deep enough to see her very soul.

'It wasn't an act—you are terrified,' he whispered. An evil grin spread across his face. 'I've got you exactly where I want you now. Would you really do anything?'

'Yes, yes, anything,' Kate sobbed. 'But please, don't leave me alone!'

His eyes were challenging. 'How about begging me to kiss you?'

'Yes, yes, anything! But please don't leave me alone.'

Enjoying himself, he prompted, 'Say, "Please kiss me, Grig".'

Kate's control returned with the strength of his presence and she found herself able to reply in kind, if a little shakily. 'You wouldn't take advantage of me like this, would you?'

'Watch me,' he answered, with a wicked, teasing grin.

'You're a . . .' A thunderclap blotted out her words, and she screamed, 'Oh, God! Hold me, Grig, please hold me!' Her burgeoning courage shattered. Her tiny hands fluttered against his chest, seeking a hold. But he pushed them aside, and they dropped useless into her lap.

'Say, "Please kiss me, Grig",' he taunted. 'I'm still not convinced you aren't acting, and I want to see how badly you want me to stay.'

'I'm not! I'm not! Why won't you believe me?' Another bolt of lightning flashed and the thunder roared its defiance.

'Well then . . .'

Shattered and terrified, and in a voice that sounded like a child begging to be forgiven, she complied. 'Please kiss me, Grig.'

He seemed to hesitate, unsure now that he had achieved his objective. But the thunder took control and she reached for him in mortal fear, begging, 'Please, please, please!'

He did—thoroughly, completely and with a feeling, at least to Kate, of punishment. Until, warming to his closeness and losing her fear in his nearness, she relaxed and her lips parted beneath his.

Then he kissed her, tenderly, his hands tangled in her hair, his lips leaving her mouth almost with regret to travel over her eyes, to trail lazily across her cheek and burn a path down her neck that Kate felt would be seen forever.

Her hands moved across his back, feeling the virile movement of his muscles as his mouth moved down her body to scald the tops of her breasts and send shivers of ice down her spine. His hands left her hair to push the flimsy nightdress away, allowing her breasts to spring free, only to be captured by his searching fingers. She heard him moan deep in his throat as his lips followed to rub gently against her throbbing nipple, encircle it and massage it with his tongue.

The angry thunder roaring in the background ceased to exist for Kate. All that existed then were his hands and lips and the fire he had lit in her veins—an all-consuming fire that burnt out any resistance and charred a need for him in her soul that no other man could erase. She stopped thinking and allowed her body to answer his, instinctively responding to his touch.

His lips recaptured hers, moving tenderly at first, then hungrily as she strained against him, her body moving with his, desperately trying to relieve with his skin the tingling sensations in her own.

Somehow, she didn't know how, and cared less, her nightdress and Grig's pyjamas had disappeared. She only wanted to lose herself in him and become a part of him. He leaned up on his elbow, gently pushing her from him.

Kate's eyes flew open to see him looking at her with a look she couldn't decipher and really didn't want to. Something told her not to reach for him as she so desperately wanted to, so she watched as he stroked her breasts almost languidly, then moved down over her hip and across her stomach. He smiled at her as he cupped her breast, stroking the nipple slowly with his thumb.

Kate's breasts felt tender and swollen, and unknowingly she thrust her body forward pushing the one he was fondling into his hand. She moaned, closing her eyes as he kneaded it gently, then reached for him and pulled him to her, searching for his mouth like a lost soul.

Grig strained against her, stroking her back as he kissed her. He cupped her buttocks, pulling her closer till she could feel him, swollen and throbbing against her thighs. His lips moved to her hair and she heard him murmur, 'It's so beautiful. Don't ever cut it off, ever.' Then his lips roved across her ear, the hot breath sending waves of delight through her as his fingers traced her side and moved to the top of her thighs, probing recesses of her body that no one had ever touched before. She stiffened and his seeking fingers stopped, his voice drifting softly into her ear.

'What is it, love?'

'I've never——' Kate sighed, then clung to him, burrowing her head into the crook of his neck.

'Never what, darling?' he asked.

But before she could answer, his searching fingers found the barrier, and he recoiled from her as if she were contaminated.

'My God!' he groaned. 'Why didn't you tell me?'

'Tell you what?' Kate wailed, wondering what she had done to make him leave her like that.

'How old are you?' he demanded, his voice dripping ice.

'I'm twenty-five,' she answered, bewildered, reaching out tentatively to touch him. But the look on his face stopped her. She felt abandoned and pulled the sheet up to cover her nakedness.

'Twenty-five and a bloody virgin! Engaged to Howard Monroe, too. Tell me, how have you managed it all these years? You're obviously not totally inexperienced. You proved that just now,' he snarled, dragging on his pyjama pants.

'I've never done anything like this before,' Kate whispered brokenly, reaching up to touch his chest, trying to reforge the bond that had been there before, then pulling back suddenly as he brushed her hand angrily away.

'Well, you certainly seemed to know what you were doing just now,' he spat.

'I didn't know what I was doing, I just . . .'

'You just *what*? Played another of your games? Designed, I suppose, to put me in my place?'

Kate's anger began to boil up. How dared he! He'd been the one to pull away, not her. She'd been so wrapped up in the sensations he had aroused in her that he could have done anything he wanted with her and she couldn't have, and wouldn't have, stopped him.

'You stopped, I didn't stop you!' she wailed at him, not knowing how to explain how he'd affected her.

'True,' he said almost to himself, 'but you would have stopped me, wouldn't you?' His expression changed to one of doubt.

'I don't think I could have stopped you even if I'd wanted to.' It was out before Kate could control her tongue.

'Well, well, well! My latent gentlemanly instincts have saved your chastity for your fiancé, haven't they?' he sneered.

'At least he wouldn't turn a girl inside out and then leave her stranded,' Kate retorted sarcastically, trying desperately to save face.

'You can bet your boots on that, my love. He wouldn't even bother to get her aroused at all if it meant wasting too much time,' Grig growled.

'What do you mean by that?' Kate screamed defiantly.

'Find out for yourself. Maybe next time there's a storm, he'll be here. See how *he* deals with your hysterics,' Grig threw back across his massive shoulder, as he stormed out, slamming the door.

Kate lay there, naked, defenceless, confused, her whole body aching for something, someone, her heart telling her that someone was Grig. She felt part of her had left with him and she didn't know why.

Oblivious to the storm that still raged outside, her mind so filled with conflicting emotions that nothing else mattered, she rolled over on to her stomach and sobbed herself to sleep, heartbroken and alone.

CHAPTER FIVE

THE flat was a mess. Kate felt *she* was a mess. The sleepless night and the emotional confrontation with Grig had drained her completely. She just wanted to go home. To hell with Grig, Darwin, and for that matter Howard. It was all too much, too much to think about and remain sane.

I've got to get out of here. This flat has too many reminders of what a fool I've been over the past couple of days, she told herself. I've got twenty-four hours to get myself together and be ready to face *that* man again if I want to stay till Howard gets back.

Maybe I should go and see Sheila Jones, Kate thought. She's pretty down-to-earth, she'll get me back to reality, I know she will. But she's a friend of Grig's, so I won't be able to talk to her about him. Still, I should be able to tell her about Howard.

Glancing at the flat and deciding that since Grig had made the mess before he'd left that morning, he should clean it up when he got back, Kate grabbed the keys to Howard's car from the kitchen bench and literally ran from the place.

She drove to the nearest service station to get petrol, and bought a map of Darwin so that she could find her way about. She located Sheila's street on her map and headed off in that direction.

She found the street and the house without too much trouble and knocked at the side door.

'Kate!' Sheila cried with delight, when she answered the door. 'I was just thinking about you. Come in.'

Kate followed her into the house and sat under the overhead fan with relief. 'I hope you aren't busy,' she said, eyeing the sewing spread out on the dining room table.

'Not really. I'm happy someone came. This dress,' Sheila fingered the material, 'isn't going right at all, and this gives me an excuse to stop.'

Sheila sprawled in the armchair opposite Kate and looked at her speculatively. 'You don't look too bright. Is the heat getting to you?'

'Not really. I had a bad night. I don't like thunderstorms,' Kate told her.

'You'll have to get used to them, I'm afraid. We get a few at this time of the year. It's the start of the wet.'

'Are they all as bad as last night's?'

'Probably not. Spike did say last night's was pretty bad. I slept through it.'

'Lucky you!'

Kate lit a cigarette and her hand shook as she put the match in the ashtray.

'You're in a bad way,' commented Sheila, noticing the shake. 'Want to tell me what the problem is, or is it too personal?'

Kate hesitated momentarily, then all her confusion came pouring out into Sheila's sympathetic ear.

'I don't know what to do!' she wailed. 'I feel
the best thing all round would be for me to get on
the next plane out of here.'

'I don't think you really want to do that, do
you? You'd never get anything sorted out that
way,' Sheila told her.

'I suppose I wouldn't. But what am I going to
do? I have to see Howard to get my thoughts
clear about how I feel. And I have to get away
from Grig. He upsets me. We seem to fight all
the time, and I really don't want to fight with
him,' Kate said plaintively.

'What do you want to do with him?' Sheila
asked.

'I wish I knew. Most of the time I want to kill
him.'

'The question is what do you want to do with
him the rest of the time?' Kate blushed crimson.
'That might not answer the question for you, but
it sure tells me a lot,' Sheila laughed.

'He's insufferable, arrogant, conceited and—
and . . .'

'You're not talking about the Grig Jacobsen I
know,' Sheila told her with a chuckle. 'You're
talking about someone else entirely.'

'You've only seen him when he's being a
perfect gentleman. You haven't seen him the way
I have.'

'Obviously not. Perhaps the trouble is that
you're two strong-willed characters both trying to
get your own way.'

'I've tried to fit in with his plans and even then
I can't seem to do the right thing,' Kate cried,
frustrated.

'Why don't you admit it to yourself,' said Sheila, seriously, in a no-nonsense voice, 'you're in love with him.'

'I'm not!' Kate broke in defensively. 'How could anyone be in love with someone as insufferable as he is? Besides, I'm in love with Howard. I hardly even know Grig.'

'For someone you hardly even know, he has a pretty drastic effect on you. Anyway, he's considered something of a catch. Most of the W.R.A.N.S. have him top of their lists and even some of the married women have set their caps at him.'

'Oh!' Kate said flatly. Her heart turned over.

'Yes—oh!' Sheila smiled. 'He's quite choosy about who he takes out, and when he does take someone out it's nothing but the best. I might add, he only takes out the best too.'

Kate's eyes glinted angrily. 'That would be typical of him, he thinks he's God's gift to the female sex.'

Sheila laughed. 'There are a whole lot of ladies round here who would agree with him.'

'How could they!' Kate stormed, thoughts of his actions the night before fanning her anger. 'He's nothing special. He's only a Lieutenant in the Navy just like Howard, and he came up through the ranks to boot.'

'Isn't that a bit snobbish?' Sheila enquired, her eyes sparkling with laughter.

'I didn't mean it to sound like that,' Kate agreed. 'But he gets me so mad, I don't know what I'm saying half the time.'

Sheila paused and looked hard at her. 'It

strikes me that it's your feelings for Grig you need to sort out. Once you've done that, how you feel about Howard will fall into place.'

Kate hesitated. 'I know how I feel about him,' she said slowly. 'I loathe him.'

Sheila's laughter made her blush and she smiled wryly knowing full well that the other woman guessed how she really felt.

'Let's forget the subject of men for the time being,' said Sheila, after she had controlled her laughter. 'Maybe what you need is some time away from both of them.'

'That's probably the most sensible idea yet,' Kate replied with relief.

Sheila rose and fetched her sewing. 'Now you're here, maybe you can help me with this thing. Here, what do you think about a frill around the neckline?'

Within minutes they were deep in discussion about fashion. The time flew and Kate forgot her problems in Sheila's company.

Kate returned to the flat feeling, if not completely sure of her feelings, at least relieved that she had been able to verbalise them to someone as understanding as Sheila. So much better did she feel that the sight of the messy and untidy abode drove her to a cleaning binge.

She was able to forget her emotional confusion in plain hard work. By six o'clock, the place sparkled. Windows gleamed and furniture shone, even the curtains had been washed. The whole flat had that air of 'a woman's touch'.

The only room she hadn't ventured into was

Grig's. Something held her back from invading
his domain. But her rising spirits brought back
some of her singlemindedness and determination
and by the time she had finished everything else,
it seemed a pity not to finish the job completely.

Heart in mouth, she picked up her cleaning
equipment and stood outside the little bedroom.
Her determination almost faltered. Damn it, she
thought, I'm only going to clean the place. He
isn't here; his room can't hurt me.

Determinedly she pushed the door open and
entered. The room smelled of his aftershave and a
wave of memory engulfed her, making her knees
weak. Pictures of his hard blue eyes staring at her
piercingly flashed across her mind and she was
forced to hang onto the door jamb for support. She
forced them from her, and telling herself not to be
stupid, she entered and began to work.

Balanced precariously on a chair, she was
replacing the freshly laundered curtains when
she heard the flat door open and her heart leaped.
Then the bedroom door burst open and she
teetered dangerously, almost losing her balance.

'What the . . .' Grig snarled angrily, taking in
her wobbling figure. 'Who gave you leave to poke
around among my personal possessions?'

He picked her up bodily and deposited her
unceremoniously on her feet facing him. His eyes
were flinty and stormy, reminding Kate of a
windblown sea.

She shivered. His hands had been none too
gentle, and she still felt the imprint of his
iron-hard fingers on her waist. Why the thought
that she wasn't exactly looking her best should

intrude she couldn't understand, but it was the most important thing to her at this moment. Shorts and shirt grubby from her afternoon's exertions, and hair bundled up in a scarf, she knew she must look a fright. Why it should worry her that Grig could find her looking her worst was a mystery, but she wanted above all to flee from his intense scrutiny and make herself look beautiful.

Defensively she tucked a stray wisp of hair back under her scarf and brought her mind away from his eyes to clutch at his words.

'I asked you why you're snooping around my room?' he snarled.

'I wasn't snooping, as you put it, I was cleaning,' Kate answered, hardly able to control the quaver in her voice.

'I see . . .' she knew from the tone that he didn't believe her, and she reddened in anger.

'Why should I poke around in your things?' she snapped back waspishly. 'I'm not in the least interested in anything to do with you!'

'Of course not,' he replied sarcastically. 'But what a perfect excuse and opportunity to find out whatever it was you were looking for. Shame I had to get back unexpectedly. Never mind, you can finish your little bit of detective work tomorrow when I'm gone. Just remember I finish at the boat at four. That way you won't get caught again.' His voice still had an edge. Kate couldn't decide whether it was still sarcasm or perhaps amusement. But whatever it was, she didn't have to take this sort of treatment from Mr High and Mighty Jacobsen.

'Go to hell!' she shouted at him. 'And in future, clean your own room!' She pushed past him, furious and bewildered—furious at him and his insinuations and bewildered at her reactions to them. She had dealt with similar reactions from recalcitrant patients when she was nursing, and had always been able to cope with it. Why did this man, with one word, manage to shatter her self-control?

He caught her arm and pulled her round to face him. 'Don't you want to know why I'm back today?'

'I really couldn't care less, and if you don't mind, I have some things to finish,' she managed to say, in what she hoped was a voice dripping with ice. To her dismay, Grig only smiled mockingly, and she jerked angrily from his grasp, flouncing out and slamming the door in, she hoped, his face.

In the kitchen, she checked the casserole she had prepared earlier and finished folding the washing. Inwardly she was seething, outwardly calm. But it was the calm of fury—fury mainly at herself for not being able to control her emotions.

I hate him, she thought. Everything was fine till he got back. I had it all sorted out in my mind, I really did, she told herself. I still do, don't I? No ... damn him, I don't. Oh God! Why does his very presence send me into a tailspin? If he'd stayed away just for one more day, I know I'd have got myself sorted out and this stupid feeling under control. Stop it, heart, she commanded, stop that thumping! I refuse to

allow a great domineering oaf like Grig Jacobsen
to confuse me and mess up my life like this.

But his mere presence in the flat sent a warm
glow through her that settled, like a giant
butterfly in the pit of her stomach, making her
dizzy, alive and somehow hypersensitive all at
the one time. She felt if he touched her now,
she would shatter into little pieces, and her
brain hated her heart for its senseless reaction
to him.

Kate knew without looking that he was behind
her. She could feel his eyes raking her back and
the fine hairs on her nape tingled electrically
almost as though he had touched her. She turned
slowly to face him.

He was watching her with a sneer on his face.
'Very domestic,' he commented, ice dripping
from each word. 'But that will have to wait till
another time. You've got half an hour to get
dressed—we're going out.'

Kate's eyes widened and her heart pounded
painfully. 'I have no desire to go out,' she stated
flatly, thankful that her voice sounded even. How
dared he presume to order her around!

'I don't want an argument, I just want you
dressed and prettied up in half an hour. We're
going to an art exhibition and dinner afterwards.
Don't argue,' Grig added, seeing her prepared to
defy him. 'Just do it.'

'I won't! I have plans for this evening. You
weren't supposed to be here, so I made
arrangements myself.' Nothing would induce her
to tell him she'd planned an evening in front of
the television set.

'Break them, then,' he ordered. 'This is important.'

'I won't. You can't make me,' she answered peevishly, her determination wilting.

'Oh, for God's sake!' he muttered with disgust. 'Please will you come with me?' He spoke as if he were addressing a child who needed to be cajoled. 'There, I've asked you nicely. If you really don't want to come,' he added slyly, 'you can cope with another storm by yourself.' He could see her resolve weaken and pressed home his advantage. 'You'd enjoy it, I promise. You'll even meet some interesting people.'

'Oh, all right.' Kate acquiesced reluctantly.

'You don't have much time now, after all that argument, so you'd better snap to it,' he ordered.

Pig, she thought, bossy pig! But her eyes sparkled as she peered at her reflection in the mirror, secretly delighted that he was back and if not exactly friendly, at least speaking to her. Speaking! His voice must be the most exciting one I've ever heard, she thought. Then deliberately putting him from her mind, which was, she found, no easy task, she jumped into the shower.

Humming softly to herself, she was busily dusting herself with her favourite talc, when Grig pounded on the bathroom door.

'Put a wriggle on, will you? I've got to get in there too!' He still sounded angry, and a little devil prodded Kate to stir his anger.

'I'll be quite a while yet,' she called sweetly. 'I have to dry my hair.' She covered her mouth to stifle a giggle, her ear at the door listening to his muffled oaths.

Wrapping herself in a bathtowel, sarong-like, she decided that while she was making him wait she'd better not waste the time completely, and began to apply her make-up.

The door from the bathroom leading to her room burst open and Grig stood there, a furious colossus. He took in her deceit at a glance. 'Lying little bitch!' he spat. 'You ought to be spanked for that, but I'll settle for you getting the hell out so I can take a shower. I'll sort you out later,' he threatened.

His hand shot out to drag her from the room, but his watch band caught the edge of her towel, and her jaw dropped when she found herself standing naked before him.

His eyes, flinty grey with anger and desire, lingered on her breasts, rosy now from the shower. Deliberately he allowed himself to take in her nakedness, enjoying the effect he was having on her.

It was almost as if his hands were on her skin, so powerful was the effect on her. She felt his eyes. She couldn't move. Her breath came in short gasps and her legs refused to obey her.

Slowly, never once letting his eyes leave her body, Grig disentangled her towel and covered her with it, his hands lingering as he fastened it at her breasts. He murmured one word that sounded to Kate like 'Later', before pushing her gently, his hand a caress on her bottom, from the room.

Trembling hands and a pounding heart made it difficult for her to dress herself and arrange her hair. But eventually she completed her toilet except for the zipper of the dress, an oyster-coloured chiffon creation that had cost her almost a week's pay. She'd been saving it for Howard, but something made her decide to wear it tonight. She knew that the low, ruffled neckline set off her full bosom to perfection and the soft, draped skirt clung tantalisingly to her hips. But her fumbling fingers managed to get the loose material of the neckline ruffle caught in the zipper. She was stuck.

She couldn't get the zip up and she couldn't get the dress off. Frustrated and angry, almost in tears, she twisted and turned, but it wouldn't budge.

Grig knocked, then entered without invitation. 'Aren't you ready yet? Or are you still playing games?'

She froze. Why did he have to find her like this? One day everything will go right when he's around, she thought. One day he'll see I'm capable of looking after myself!

'Hold still. I'll fix that,' he ordered.

His hands were gentle as he carefully dis-entangled the material and freed the zipper. Kate revelled in his touch, hating herself for her reaction. He pulled the zip into place and stroked the material into its folds. Finished, he planted a light kiss on the nape of her neck, sending shivers of delight down her spine and sending her heart spinning.

'There ... fixed,' he said, turning her round. 'You'll do. Let's go.'

His matter-of-fact tone and the carefully blank expression on his face sent her spirits plummeting. How could he turn her emotions round like that. He felt nothing for her, and yet she was reacting to his lips like some little schoolgirl with a crush. Grown women don't fall for men who don't feel at least a little something for them. Not if they're sensible anyway, she admonished herself. All this great chauvinist wants is a quick romp in the hay, so he can put another star on his score sheet, she thought shrewishly as she followed him to the car. But a little voice kept whispering, if that was true then why did he stop the night of the storm? She couldn't have stopped him. She hadn't wanted to stop him and even now, she was guilty, because deep down she wished he hadn't.

One thing's for sure, she told herself, pushing the little voice aside, her shattered composure returning, Sheila was dead wrong. I'm not in love with him and never will be. He might be some girl's idea of Mr Right, but not mine.

She couldn't understand why the butterfly in her stomach refused to sleep, but lurched and fluttered when his hand brushed her knee as he changed gears.

They pulled up outside a modern brick building just outside the centre of the city. A well-known airline's logo was prominently displayed above the entrance. People were entering in tight little clutches, and curious as she was, Kate refused to ask him where they were or what the occasion.

Grig cupped his hand under her elbow to escort her in, but she pulled away, still angry with his treatment of her and still unsure she could cope with the storm of emotion that his touch would bring.

She glanced at him and her eyes sparkled with an excitement she couldn't conceal. He was so handsome, so male, so very sure of himself. Even dressed casually in a light safari suit, he carried himself like a man who knew he was desirable to women, and Kate's heart leaped to think that, even though it wasn't from choice on his part, she was still the woman he was with tonight.

They stopped at the door to allow another couple to enter and Grig leant down to whisper in her ear, 'You'll wow them, love. You've glowing!'

She looked up to see his eyes taking in the flush of excitement on her cheeks. 'Don't fight me now,' he breathed, 'save it for later.' He cupped his hand once more under her elbow and the electric tingle of his touch made her eyes sparkle even brighter. Kate allowed it to remain and her feet scarcely touched the floor, so right did it feel. Unconsciously she held her head high and strutted, like a woman who knew she was exactly where she belonged.

A strident voice brought her back to earth. 'Kate! Kate Rhodes. You didn't tell me you were coming to Darwin!'

Kate's head spun round to see the tall, lithe figure of Nola Stevens bearing down on her through the crowd. 'Hello, Nola. I didn't know you were coming either, or I would have. How long will you be here?'

'Oh, I've managed to get myself sent up to

work in the office here for a few days. Ground duties makes a break from flying anyway, and at least I'll have time to see a bit of the place. Stopovers don't really give one the opportunity to sightsee.'

Kate looked round to introduce Nola to Grig, but he'd disappeared into the crowd. Nola was an air hostess that she and Howard knew from Sydney and though not a good friend was more than a casual aquaintance.

'What brings you here tonight?' Nola enquired, in her breathless, gushy voice that matched her dizzy style to perfection.

Before Kate could reply, Grig joined them, holding two glasses of wine.

'Grig, darling!' she gushed. 'Surely *you* two aren't together? Where's Howard?'

'Hello, Nola,' said Grig, somewhat grimly, Kate thought. 'I didn't know you two were acquainted.'

'We met in Sydney and have mutual friends,' Kate answered for her.

'I was just thinking about you earlier,' Nola told Kate, ignoring Grig. 'Since you gave me Howard's phone number I've tried to reach him every time I've passed through, but we always seem to miss one another. I tried to reach him today, but it seems he's away again. Pity.'

Grig made a strangled sound and Kate turned to see him busily pulling his handkerchief from his pocket. 'Sorry, ladies,' he gasped. 'Drink went down the wrong way.'

'Grig's kindly showing me round while Howard's at sea,' Kate told Nola, giving Grig a sly glance to see if he'd notice the sarcastic inflection in her voice.

'Lucky you,' drawled Nola, batting her long false eyelashes at him. 'Perhaps he'll show *me* round when Howard gets back.'

'I've a feeling, Nola dear, that I'll be pretty tied up for quite a while,' Grig threw back at her. Kate noticed his jaw tense.

'Like that, is it, Grig darling?' asked Nola, her eyes wide.

Grig glared at her, and in a hard, flat voice said, 'Yes, Nola, it is. And I would appreciate it, my love, if you would remember what I told you last time we met.'

Kate felt the tension between them but couldn't understand it. Nola's reaction to his words made her suspect that they held some sort of warning or threat, but what she couldn't tell. Still, she thought, it isn't any of my business.

'Let me get you a drink, Nola,' Grig said calmly, and the tension eased as he left the two girls together.

Nola watched him push through the crowd. 'Arrogant swine, isn't he?' she said conversationally. 'How do you stand him?'

'Oh, I don't take him too seriously,' Kate replied, unable to meet the other girl's eyes.

'Tell you what, Kate,' Nola said conspiratorially, 'I'm having a party tomorrow night at some friends' house. Why not come along? That is if you aren't already going somewhere,' she added with a hint of malice. 'Or should I say if you can get away from the almighty Grig Jacobsen.'

'Nola, he's just doing Howard a favour looking after me till Howard gets back. I don't have to do anything he tells me,' Kate answered, puzzled by Nola's tone. 'I'll come if I can. In fact, I'd love to. Can I let you know for sure tomorrow?' she asked.

'Don't worry about that. Just come if you can. Here, I'll give you the address.' Nola pulled a notebook from her bag and hastily scrawled an address on it. She tore the page off and pushed it at Kate. 'Here, I'll see you later.' She was gone in a whirl of skirt and a cloud of pungent perfume.

Grig returned with another wine. 'Gone already?' he asked cheerfully. Kate felt he was happy to see her go and didn't mention the party. He may not be here tomorrow night, so I won't have to tell him, she thought, surprised at herself for not wanting to tell him. Somehow she felt he wouldn't approve.

'Let's look at the paintings,' he said, taking her elbow again and guiding her skilfully through the crush to where the art work was displayed.

The paintings were tastefully arranged along the far wall of the room, some on the wall, some on easels, but all striking in their intensity. One in particular caught Kate's eye—a large, vivid seascape emitting a strong, virile image. The sea almost jumped from the canvas and the gulls were so real that Kate felt she could hear their cries.

'Grig!' she gasped, in delight. 'It's Fanny Bay, just like we see it from the balcony of the flat. Oh, Grig, it's beautiful! Is it for sale? Can I afford it, do you think?'

'Why don't you look at the rest first?' he said in amusement. 'There might be something else you like better.'

'Are they all for sale?' she asked him.

'Yes, they are. This is a private showing that the airline agreed to hold here in their building, mainly because the manager is a friend of the artist and a percentage of the sales are going to charity.'

'They're all so wonderful—vivid and strong. The artist must have a very strong personality for it to come through in his paintings like this.'

'If I'd said that,' he laughed, 'you'd have called me a male chauvinist.'

Wandering among the pictures, Kate lost herself in the painter's world and a feeling of knowing him overtook her. Not knowing him as a person, but knowing him in a way she couldn't explain. He seemed able through his work to bring an understanding of the subjects he had chosen to his audience.

The subjects were mainly seascapes, but dotted among them were some wonderfully emotive paintings of birds. Birds like the ones she and Grig had watched near Humpty Doo.

Almost at the very end of the room was a smaller, more subdued canvas that took Kate's breath away. It was a painting of a pair of brolgas dancing. It had a sensual quality about it, tender almost, and she looked at the painting next to it to compare the artist's signature. In the corner of each was a scrawled set of initials that she could only decipher as G. J.

Now sure that the same person had painted

both, she looked again at the brolgas. She felt that the artist had bared a part of his soul that was hidden in his seascapes. His others were strong, determined, virile, while the brolgas showed a softer, almost vulnerable quality, like the reverse side of a coin. This man must be very complex, Kate thought, and I'll bet as a lover he'd be magnificent. She flushed, never before had she wondered about a complete stranger's lovemaking ability and now to be thinking this way about someone she'd never even met confused her.

Still, she thought, if his paintings have that sort of effect on people, it only shows how good he must be. She felt relieved that she'd been able to rationalise her feelings.

She searched with her eyes through the crowd for Grig who had left her to look at the paintings alone. Perhaps the artist is here, she thought, and Grig might know him. I'd love to meet someone who can paint like that.

She found him engrossed in conversation with a man she'd never seen before and burrowed through the press to his side, determined to ask him to help her organise the purchase of the brolgas. Moving closer, not wanting to intrude, she caught the stranger's words, 'When are you going to give up the Navy and paint full-time, Grig? You know now you can do it and make a damn good living at it.'

'Maybe one day. It's a hobby and I enjoy it, but I still don't know if I could do it full-time.'

'You're mad,' the stranger told him. 'Look at the prices they're fetching now! That fellow from

the Sydney gallery over there says he can sell as
many as you can give him, and he even
mentioned a contract for supplying a number for
a very well-known interior decorating firm, who
do a lot of the really big decorating jobs here and
in New Zealand. You'd never go broke, and I
think you'd end up making a fortune.'

Kate couldn't believe her ears. Grig was the
artist! Now she knew why she felt she knew who
had done the paintings, but she couldn't imagine
him putting such feelings into the brolgas.
Obviously there was a side to Grig Jacobsen that
he kept well hidden.

He caught her eye and excused himself,
stepping over to her. 'Like another drink?'

'Grig, these paintings are yours,' she told him,
amazed.

'Uh-huh,' he mumbled, almost shyly. 'My
hobby.'

'But they're marvellous! You could be a full-
time artist if you wanted.'

'One day I will. At the moment it's a rather
lucrative sideline. Come on, let's mingle a little,
then we'll go for dinner.'

Kate stifled the comments she had about his
work, aware that he didn't want to continue with
the subject, only telling him that she would like
to buy the painting of the brolgas. He left her for
a moment to say something to the man he had
been speaking to, and when he returned he told
her it had been arranged and she saw the man put
a 'sold' sign on it.

'You won't get it for a couple of days,' Grig
explained. 'They'll be here till the weekend.'

'I'd better pay someone, hadn't I?' she queried.

'I told you it was fixed,' he said, a little angrily, and Kate forbore to take the matter further, determined to speak to him about the payment when he was a little easier to approach.

They left the showing shortly after and Grig took her to a fairly new seafood restaurant close to where the showing was held. It was close enough for them to walk and he held her hand lightly as they strolled through the deserted Darwin streets.

Kate's mind was full—full of the pictures, full of feelings she knew not how to deal with and really didn't want to. Not now at least. His hand in hers was warm and her skin thrilled to his touch. She tried to pretend that it meant nothing, and knowing it meant nothing to him was still somehow content for such a minimal show of affection. The thought crossed her mind that, along with her painting, this small interlude would be a memory she could cherish in the years to come, a memory known to her alone and held dearly in her heart. Maybe one day, she'd be able to tell her own daughter about it when the time came. Realising that she was somehow planning a life without this man didn't shock her. She'd known all along that there would be no life with him, and she planned to store up all the memories of him that she could.

It was strangely comforting to have settled that in her mind, a paradox, she thought. Still, life must go on, and Kate could not envisage a life without a family, and for that she would have to accept second best. She smiled a secret smile.

Second best, she did love him; Sheila was right.
Perhaps it was as well that Howard was still
there. The best way to put him from her mind
would be with Howard. But tonight she was
going to accept her feelings and enjoy the
presence of the one man in the world she could
love with all her heart. Howard or whoever took
his place would just have to be content with
whatever part she had left, for there would always
be a large part of her heart reserved solely for
Grig.

Stupid, stupid, she berated herself when she
realised the way her mind was running. You
don't love him. The tropics have got to you.
Wake up, girl, you've got tropical fever and
you're delirious. She pulled her hand from his,
breaking the contact that had the power to turn
her head into a dream world and away from the
reality of life.

I mustn't let him touch me again, she decided.
All I feel for him is purely physical, and love is
more than that. Love is more like Howard and I
have. Something more. What would Grig and I
have if the physical died? she asked. Nothing.
Nothing. I don't even like him, and he can't
abide me most of the time.

Their arrival at the Rock Oyster interrupted
her chain of thought and much to her own
amusement, she was glad to be able to put her
musings aside and concentrate on everyday
things. Grig settled her at the table and excused
himself for a while to go across the road to buy a
bottle of wine. The restaurant was a B. Y. O. and,
he explained, he hadn't wanted to take her into a

hotel bottle shop. Kate didn't mind and sat happily watching the other diners. The place was crowded and she realised he must have booked earlier, for quite a few people who came in were being turned away.

He returned and gave the waitress the wine, then joined her at the little table for two in the far corner. It was dim and somehow apart from the other larger tables, and the candlelight set a romantic atmosphere.

They spoke little during the entree of succulent fresh oysters, and Grig seemed content not to push the conversation, he seemed happy just to relax and eat. Once his fingers brushed hers as he poured her wine and she looked up to see him watching her closely, but she pulled away and he made no comment.

The menu was extensive and varied, and she accepted his suggestion that she would have a chance to try a variety of the local seafood if they had the platter. It was a meal for two, consisting of all the seafood imaginable, and she was happy to agree with him.

Sitting over the debris of the meal, Kate decided to at least attempt to talk a little. Searching for a topic that would be safe, she asked about his painting. 'I haven't seen any painting things at the flat. Don't you keep any there?'

'I keep them on the boat. That's where I get most of my inspiration, so that's where I paint.'

'What about the birds?' Kate asked, surprised.

'Sometimes I take a few things out to the bush and start something there, then I take it back and finish it on board.'

'Isn't that a bit hard on board?' she asked, trying to keep the conversation moving. He seemed loath to talk at all.

'I only paint when we're at anchor somewhere,' he said, then as if he felt he needed to explain to her he added, 'I love the sea. That's why I'm in the Navy. That's why I paint it. I'll never lose my love of it.' He stopped suddenly, and took a gulp of his wine. It was almost, Kate thought, as though he had bared part of his soul to her. He seemed to have said the words with difficulty, as if they had been dragged from an unwilling mind.

'Speaking of the Navy,' said Kate, 'I forgot to ask why you came back so soon?'

Grig's face closed, his eyes glinted with anger. 'Problems,' he said flatly.

'I'm sorry,' she said. She could think of nothing else to say, and his expression told her to ask would invite his anger.

'We'd better leave,' he snarled. 'I have to work tomorrow.'

He signalled for the bill and hustled her from the restaurant. Now what have I done? Kate wondered. We seemed to be getting on quite well. He's impossible—and I'd been imagining that I loved him. What a joke!

They walked back to the car, silent, carefully avoiding contact. Grig didn't even help her in, but opened her door from the driver's side and allowed her to get in herself. They drove home in silence, a silence that was almost tangible. One word, Kate thought, would be enough to set off an explosion. But she still didn't know why.

Her anger flared as they arrived back at the flat

and her mind was racing as they went in. I won't be treated like this, she thought, not by him or anyone else. Howard wouldn't treat me like this, so why should Grig? The least he could do is tell me what I'm supposed to have done.

She threw her bag on a chair and turned stormy eyes to him. Hands on hips, she confronted him. 'I've never met anyone as impossible as you!' she cried. 'One minute you're almost human, the next you clam up like an oyster, and I don't even know why or what I've done. If I've said something wrong, you could tell me.'

He looked at her coldly. 'You,' he said, emphasising the pronoun, 'didn't say anything wrong. Just forget it and go to bed.'

'Go to hell!' she spat, not knowing how else to reply. If she hadn't said something wrong what on earth had made him so silent? 'Well, you won't have to save me from imaginary storms tomorrow night,' she added, spitefully. 'I'm going to a party at Nola's.'

Suddenly he was towering over her. 'What did you say?' he asked in a hard, cruel voice.

'I'm going to Nola's,' she repeated, pleased somehow that she'd shaken him out of his sullen inwardness, even if it was into anger.

'Not if I have anything to do with it,' he stated flatly.

'You've got nothing to do with it. I'll go if I please!' She turned, but he pulled her back, taking her chin in a vice-like grip, forcing her face up so that their eyes met. His eyes bored into hers and his grip softened and became almost caressing. 'You won't like Nola's party. Take my word for it, I don't want you to go.'

Kate felt the butterfly begin his dance again and wanted to sway towards him. It took all her willpower to stop her legs from trembling and to keep her voice steady. 'Let me go,' she demanded. 'You've no right to order me around. I'll do as I please and you won't stop me.'

'Oh, will you?' he demanded.

'Yes, I will,' defiance in her voice.

His hand left her chin and he pinioned her with his arms, picking her up bodily and folding her easily across his knees as he sat in the nearby chair.

'I warned you about being cheeky. That also applied to defiant, and I seem to recall that there was something left undone owing to pressure of time. Well, it's time we rectified that,' he taunted her with the first slap.

Kate kicked and bit her lip. I won't scream, she moaned to herself, I won't. He won't make me. I'll kill him, just as soon as he lets me go. I'll kill him! The spanking was more humiliating than painful, but her composure was shattered.

She was beside herself with rage when he released her and, spitting like a cat, clawed at his face, incoherent with anger. Grig easily imprisoned her raking fingers and pulled her roughly back on to his lap.

'Cat!' he laughed. 'I know one good way of dealing with a woman when she gets like this.' His lips closed over hers, hard, demanding, cruel, burning, ravishing her mouth and searing her soul.

She fought him silently, tearing at his shirt, clawing at his chest, leaving red weals on the sun-bronzed skin. But nothing she did stopped his lips. He became demanding, forcing her lips to open and her mouth to surrender to his. Her lips moved with a will of their own against his and her hands relaxed to stroke the scratch marks and caress the weals.

Moaning in ecstasy, Kate moved against him, tangling her fingers in the mat of golden hair on his chest. His kisses softened and his mouth moved hungrily down her neck, then back again to nibble at the dimple beside her mouth.

Warmth spread through her body, settling in her loins, and her lips searched hungrily for his mouth. His vice-like grip relaxed and his hands moved gently over her, cupping her breast through the soft material of her dress, teasing the already rigid nipple. He pushed impatiently at the fabric till the soft white globe sprung free and his lips were able to possess it.

His lips left her breast and he kissed her eyes, while his hands tugged at the combs holding her hair. 'Shake your head,' he commanded huskily. She did and her hair cascaded down to form a dark, silken curtain that enfolded them both.

His face and hands were in her hair, revelling in its silken luxury. Tugging, stroking, kissing it, he moaned deep in his throat. 'I want you,' he groaned, before his mouth once more took possession of her love-bruised lips and his hand claimed her aching breast.

CHAPTER SIX

KATE'S head ached and she sat in front of the bedroom mirror, eyes closed. The tablets she had taken an hour ago were taking longer than usual to work. She massaged her temples in the hope that the gentle rubbing would ease the tension. Tension, and why not? Anyone would be tense after last night's fiasco.

Fiasco was the word, no doubt about that, she thought. Her temples pounded harder and she tried to push away the mental images that spun behind her eyes. Images that shamed her. Shamed and excited all at the same time.

Oh, how could I let myself get carried away like that? she moaned. It was my own fault, I know, and if I'm truthful, probably for the best. Her mind swung back to the night before, reliving each moment.

'I want you,' Grig moaned huskily. He picked her up bodily and she snuggled in his arms, pressing her love-bruised lips to his neck.

She was happy, light, safe, secure, wanted, loved. Every happy emotion spun around inside her head like a kaleidoscope. What had possessed her to tease him then? She would never know. But the words had tumbled out happily amidst the laughter.

'Can I go to Nola's party now?'

His reaction stunned her, shook her to the core,

showed her a side of him she had never dreamed existed. She had seen him angry, silent, arrogant and at times even tender, but never this raging tumultuous fury.

He almost threw her on the floor. She fell huddled against the bedroom door, watching him awestruck through the dark curtain of her hair, a screen that covered her nakedness and her hurt.

Hands on hips, he surveyed her like a man watching something foul. Kate felt the hate bounce off her and shivered. His look was despising and she felt if she moved he might be tempted to kill her. 'Teasing bitch,' he spat. 'Another of your acts?'

She shook her head, mute, her heart crying no, no!

'Thank God it happened now. I think I might have killed you if it had happened later.' His words meant nothing. Only the loathing touched her.

'What did I do?' she sobbed in despair.

'Don't give me that! You know exactly what you did. I suppose you tease Howard like that to get your own way. How far do you go before you call a halt?' His words cut through her like a knife.

'I didn't mean anything,' Kate wailed, her head pressed against the bedroom door, shoulders shaking. 'I wasn't teasing.' Her words came jerking out torn from her battered heart.

He reached down and took a handful of her hair. She flinched as he tugged it, pulling her up to her feet. His jaw was set and a pulse pounded at the base of his throat.

Kate cringed away from this mountain of fury. 'I'm sorry, I'm sorry, don't hurt me,' she begged. 'Whatever I've done to make you angry, I'm sorry.'

Grig jerked her head up to search her face with his hard blue eyes. His look softened and his eyes held hers for a heart-stopping moment.

'God, what a fool!' he murmured to himself. His voice was surprisingly gentle, as he stroked her cheek, 'You really don't know what's happening, do you? Poor little naïve kitten.' His hands cupped her head and his fingers stroked her tangled hair. 'Forgive me, pet. I'm not used to dealing with girls like you. I know that won't be much consolation, but some day you'll understand. But then again, perhaps you'll never understand.' He spoke almost to himself, and Kate's brain whirled, trying to make sense of it all.

'Don't hate me, try to forget this ever happened.' He brushed his lips gently across her hair. 'Go to bed, kitten.' He stopped her words with his finger. 'Don't argue,' he whispered, 'Just do it. Go to Nola's tomorrow if you really want to. I'll be here if you need me.'

He turned on his heel and left her. Kate stumbled to her room and collapsed, distraught, on the bed.

Kate's mind returned to the present. She knew that now she would have to go to the party, regardless of how she felt. She had to show him she wasn't some half-grown schoolgirl who needed a chaperone. She had to smile and pretend last night had never happened—God knows how. She'd never forget it as long as she lived; somehow she didn't want to.

She took two more aspirins from the bottle before her, laid the dress she had chosen to wear on the bed, then went to see if a long cool shower could revive her.

The taxi deposited Kate outside the address she had given Grig in Casuarina. The house was brightly lit and she could hear the sound of pop music blaring from a hi-fi set.

She stood for a moment after the taxi had gone, a little afraid to go in by herself. She did a mental check on her appearance. Emerald green jersey, halter-necked dress, falling in soft folds to calf-length. Perhaps a little too dressy for Darwin. Hair up in a soft coil, off her neck for coolness. Not too sophisticated, she decided. High-heeled strappy sandals, green to match the dress. Any other shoes would have spoiled the effect of the dress's hemline. Oh well, mother had always said, 'better to be over than under-dressed'.

Squaring her shoulders and taking a deep breath of the salt-laden air, she strode determinedly into the garden.

She followed the sounds of the party to the pool, where about twenty people were milling about, some talking, some dancing shoeless on the lawn, and others already swimming. She was relieved to see that most of the women were similarly dressed to her, although perhaps a little more casually. So, before anyone could notice, she turned into the darkness behind a frangipani shrub and removed her necklace and earrings,

which gave her outfit the lift it needed to make it
suitable for a dinner dress, and popped them into
her bag. Then she quickly removed the pins
holding her hair in place, and allowed it to
tumble free. She shook her head and smoothed
the front of it with her hands. Then, satisfied that
she looked casual enough, she strolled into the
light, looking for her hostess.

Kate spotted Nola holding court at the
opposite side of the pool and catching her eye,
gave a wave. Nola excused herself from the group
she was with and made her way to Kate.

Kate watched her friend coming towards her,
admiring her outfit. Nola, always elegant, looked
particularly fetching in a floor-length white
wrap-round skirt, swirled all over with various
shades of pink, pale at the waist deepening to a
vivid ruby at the hem. Her skirt was teamed with
a white bikini top that Kate surmised had
matching briefs requiring only the removal of the
skirt for Nola to be ready to swim. The skirt
swished seductively as she walked and the
combination of white, mahogany-tanned skin and
platinum-blonde hair drew many admiring stares.

'You made it, Kate. Great!' Nola gushed in her
usual breathless way, as she steered Kate towards
a group of people.

'Everyone . . . this is Kate Rhodes, a friend of
mine from Sydney. Kate, meet everyone!' Nola
screamed above the music and babble of voices,
setting Kate's teeth on edge.

Kate remembered Nola's habit of screeching
when she had had a few drinks and looking
round, it was apparent everyone at the party had

been drinking for some time. It looked as if it wasn't going to be her sort of party at all. But regardless, she thought, she would stay. She couldn't go home to the flat now to have Grig say 'I told you so'.

She made her way over to a makeshift bar that had been set up beside the pool and helped herself to a glass of wine. Standing surveying the crowd, she sipped it slowly, wondering what she could do to pass the time till she could make her excuses and leave without hurting Nola's feelings or getting home too early so that Grig would laugh at her.

She stood watching the groups break, mix and re-form. Each group revolved round a brilliantly clad girl. They reminded her of flowers surrounded by honey bees, and the men moved between the groups like bees dipping for honey at different blooms, unable to make up their minds which one was the sweetest. Kate pondered on the scarcity of women at the party, and then recalled someone telling her that in the Territory, men outnumbered women by about ten to one. It would make for an interesting social life for single girls, she mused. Now she knew why Nola and her fellow hostesses vied for the Darwin run.

Within minutes of her arrival, Kate was herself surrounded by her own group of male admirers, and she began to enjoy the attention, even though, at heart, she wasn't a flirt. But regardless of any misgivings she might have, she threw herself into the game in a conscious effort to prove to herself—and in a strange way, Grig?— that she was capable of handling this sort of situation.

A very young-looking man in shorts and a
bright floral shirt pushed his way into the group
around her.

'Listen, you guys,' he said, addressing the
others generally. 'This lady, and you all can see,
I'm sure, that she *is* a lady, is an old friend of
mine. So if you wouldn't mind, I'm going to
monopolise her for a while.'

His remarks brought murmurs of dissent from
the other men. But he continued, 'Come on,
fellows, give an old friend a break. We haven't
seen each other for ages. You wouldn't deny me
half an hour. After all, the night's still a pup.
There'll be plenty of time for you to move in
later.'

'But I've never met you before in my life,'
Kate exclaimed, as the others moved off to
mingle with other guests.

'Of course you haven't,' he laughed. 'But you
can't blame a guy for trying to beat everybody's
time, when beautiful ladies like you are so
scarce.'

She flushed as he guided her away from the bar
to a dim corner near a fragrant hibiscus, plucked
one of the scarlet blooms and tucked it behind
her left ear.

'I hope that's the correct ear,' he whispered. 'I
can never remember which one it is means the
lady is spoken for.'

'I thought that was a Polynesian custom,' Kate
replied, moving towards the light and relative
safety. 'Anyway, I'm already spoken for, as you
so charmingly put it.'

'Who's the lucky man?' her companion asked,

looking around to see if any jealous boy-friends were descending on them.

'You probably wouldn't know him. And you can stop looking, he's not here,' Kate smiled.

'Thank heavens for that! But you must think I'm a real nut, pulling a stunt like that without even telling you my name. Peter McCann, at your service,' he said, obviously relieved.

'How do you do, Pete McCann,' said Kate, feeling more secure since she had manoeuvred them back to the bar. 'I'm Kate—Kate Rhodes.'

'I'm very pleased to meet you, Kate Rhodes,' said Pete, putting a strong emphasis on the 'very'.

Kate sipped her drink reflectively, wondering why she had a creeping feeling of dread about this apparently charming man. She could accept his fabrication about knowing her before and smile at his inventiveness. But somehow there seemed to be an underlying menace in his breezy manner.

'It's nice to see another beautiful new hostie on the Darwin run, even if she is spoken for,' he said. 'But somehow I don't think you'll be that way for long if you keep making this run. None of them do.'

'Oh?' said Kate, leaving the question hang, hoping for enlightenment without giving too much information herself.

'You must be fairly new at the game,' he hinted. 'All the girls know that engagements falter after a couple of Darwin runs, and I can't see you being any exception.'

'Do I seem that conformist?' Kate asked, smiling, knowing full well she had information he didn't and revelling in the secret knowledge.

'It isn't that, exactly,' he told her. 'It's just that you're more than average looking, nice to talk to, and have that air of 'fire and ice' that will drive the women-starved male population here mad.'

Kate smiled at the flattery, and her mind flew back to the day on Grig's boat when he had called her frozen, then set about proving she wasn't. She told herself to stop thinking about him, but everything now seemed to remind her of something he had said or done, and she felt herself trapped in a web of emotions she couldn't control. She determined she *would* control them. Grig Jacobsen was an arrogant devil, who was determined to prove he could take any woman he saw. But she would show him he couldn't have her. Then her mind fastened on the night of the storm, and blushing, she had to admit to herself he could have had her then and, truth to tell, now if he really tried.

Damn him, she thought, the sooner Howard gets back and we get everything back to normal, the better. I won't feel this way after I've seen Howard, she told herself.

But somewhere in the back of her mind the knowledge that she was lying to herself niggled, and she put it back bitterly into the 'too hard' slot.

Looking up from her drink, she noticed Pete smiling and realised that he thought her blush was the result of his flattery, which made her flush deeper. She was unaware how the reddening of her cheeks added a dimension to her looks that was almost breathtaking. But he had not missed it.

Bringing her thoughts back to the conversation, Kate asked wryly,' How will that affect my relationship with my fiancé?'

'Easy. Most men tak a dim view of their women being squired round by hosts of other men while they're a couple of thousand miles away. And besides, most of the girls eventually take the view of not tying themselves down to one man, when they can have their pick of so many.'

'I can see where some girls might take that attitude,' Kate laughed. 'But you see, I'm not a hostess. I'm just a friend of Nola's from Sydney, who happens to be in Darwin to see her fiancé. So I don't fit any of your categories, do I?'

'Well, if that's the case,' said Pete, in a manner that made Kate suspect he didn't believe a word she'd said, 'where is he? If it was me, I wouldn't be letting someone like you out on their own in Darwin. Certainly not to one of these bashes.'

'If you must know,' Kate replied, 'he's out on patrol at the moment and will be back in a few days. And anyway, what's wrong with these bashes, as you call them?'

Pete looked stunned for a moment, then recovering, laughed nervously, as he poured them both another drink.

'He's in the Navy, then, I take it?' he asked.

'Yes, on one of the boats,' Kate answered, rather pleased to see Pete so put out. 'Does that make a difference?'

'No, no . . . It's just that most of the men here are navy types from the boats and Coonawarra.'

'Coonawarra?' Kate queried.

'Yes, that's the base here,' he explained.

'Maybe some of the people will know Howard,' said Kate. 'That is, besides Nola.'

'Nola knows him, then?' Pete asked.

'Yes. We both knew Nola in Sydney. That's how I was invited here tonight. I gave Nola Howard's phone number a while ago and told her he was here. She's been trying to reach him for a while when she's been up here before. Anyway, I ran into her last night at a party. So here I am.'

'Howard? That wouldn't be Howard Monroe, would it?' Pete asked.

'Yes. Do you know him?'

Kate was surprised at the reaction to her question. Pete turned away coughing, but she could see his shoulders shaking and knew that the coughing fit was to cover a burst of laughter. She didn't know quite what to do.

Pete turned to face her, red-faced and grinning.

'Sorry about that,' he gulped, taking her by the elbow and guiding her to a group standing near the pool. 'Hey, folks,' he called as they approached, 'guess who this is!'

Heads turned to stare at them and Kate felt her cheeks burning. Damn it all, she thought, all I seem to do since I've come to this God forsaken hole called Darwin is cry, blush and generally let my emotions run riot. I'm acting like a kid, and I've got to snap out of it.

'It's Howard Monroe's fiancée,' Pete added, still grinning.

Nola detached herself from the man she was with and hurried over to Kate.

'Come on now, lay off! Kate's here to see

Howard, nothing wrong with that, is there?' she
said with what Kate felt was unusual savagery.

'Why should Pete think it's funny?' Kate
asked.

'Just don't take any notice of him; he's a bit of
a stirrer,' Nola replied.

Kate could still feel eyes following her and she
felt very selfconscious. She felt as if everyone was
laughing at her for reasons she couldn't fathom
and her selfconsciousness increased, making her
spill her drink. 'Oh dear, look what I've done!'
she cried to Nola. 'I'll have to go home now, I
can't stay here like this.'

'Don't worry about it,' Nola replied. 'Come
upstairs and I'll lend you a swimsuit, you can go
for a dip while your dress dries.'

Loath to let all these people see that their
behaviour had affected her, and equally loath to
return to the flat and Grig's 'I told you so', Kate
complied. Nola lent her a very becoming black
bikini, which set off her milk-white skin and the
cut of which emphasised her tiny waist and well
proportioned legs.

While she changed, Nola sponged her dress
and hung it in a doorway where the breeze could
dry it.

'Come on, let's go for a swim,' Nola said,
slipping out of her patio skirt to reveal, as Kate
had suspected, the remainder of her swimsuit.

'Fine by me,' answered Kate, feeling far from
fine, but determined to carry the evening off
successfully, at all costs.

The sight of two such opposite but attractive
girls in brief swimwear, complementing each

other, brought conversation almost to a halt as they sauntered to the pool and dived in.

The water was warm but refreshing and Kate wallowed in the unusual luxury of an evening swim. Floating peacefully on her back, oblivious to the poolside chatter, she watched the stars. She was surprised once more, as she had been from her first night in the Territory, at their brilliance. But her musings were interrupted by screams and splashes as almost the whole company joined her and Nola in the pool. It was as if their dip were the signal for the start of the aquatic high jinks that followed.

Kate was far from happy at the change in proceedings, and clambered out. She dried herself off and fetching another drink from the bar, sat in a chair, far enough from the water to escape the jets thrown up by the revellers, and settled down to watch the fun. She was just beginning to think that the evening might not be as bad as she had suspected at first, when Pete, dripping and breathless from laughing, plopped down in a chair beside her. Kate felt her initial uneasy feeling about him return.

'Aren't you going back in?' he asked, swallowing half his drink in one go. Kate noticed he had changed from wine to spirits, and her sense of unease increased.

'No, I'm quite happy just watching,' she said.

'Well, if you won't swim, let's dance,' he said, grabbing her hand and pulling her out of the chair and into his arms.

Not wanting to cause a scene, Kate allowed him to dance with her, pulling away so that their bodies didn't touch. But he was more drunk than she thought, and her manoeuvre only served to stave off his amorous gropings for a moment.

'Come on, he's not here tonight,' he slurred, jerking her towards him and planting a wet, liquor-smelling kiss on her face.

Kate pushed at him in disgust, slapping his groping hands away.

'Don't be a party pooper,' he leered, grabbing at her again. 'Howard won't mind, I'm sure.'

'How would you know what Howard would mind?' she demanded, desperately trying to avoid his grasp, and almost sending him sprawling with a particularly hefty push.

Pete recovered his footing and stood looking at her with what amounted to amazement. 'You can't be that naïve,' he said, 'and besides, you said you knew about Nola.'

'Knew about Nola?' Kate asked bewildered. 'What about Nola?'

It was apparent that Pete, regardless of his drunken condition, had realised he'd made a faux pas. 'Nothing. Don't mind me, I was only joking,' he said repentantly. 'Come on, I promise I'll behave. Let's have that dance.'

'No, I think I'll sit down for a while,' said Kate, and matching words to actions, strode angrily back to her seat at the poolside.

Out of the corner of her eye she could see Pete downing his drink and pouring himself another, which quickly followed it, to be replaced immediately by yet another. She knew he was annoyed with her but she decided to ignore him. If he wanted to get drunk, she thought, that was his business.

Her attention was drawn by loud screams of laughter, to the antics in the pool, and she looked at the swimmers to see what was causing all the commotion. Her mouth dropped open in a mixture of shock and distaste.

The game, apparently, was to remove the girl's bikini tops, and most of them were already topless—and, from what Kate could see, enjoying it. The loudest screams were coming from Nola, who was being chased by two of the men, intent on removing the rest of her costume. It was obvious to Kate that Nola wasn't trying too hard to escape, and with a look of disgust she rose from her chair, determined to recover her clothes from the house and leave the scene immediately.

She found her way barred by the belligerent form of Pete McCann, now very much the worse for drink and bent on mischief.

'Let's join the fun,' he said, a sordid look in his eyes.

'No, thanks, Pete, I'm going home,' Kate said quietly, in a vain effort to avoid a scene.

He snickered and a viscious gleam appeared in his drink-sodden eyes. 'You can't go home yet. Not till you've shown Howard's Darwin girl-friend that you've just as much to offer as she has.'

'What do you mean, Pete? Howard's *Darwin* girl-friend?' Kate asked, trying to avoid his wandering hands.

'Nola, of course. Everyone knows about Howard and Nola,' he muttered drunkenly, grabbing at her bikini top.

'Let me go, you drunken swine!' Kate snapped, still attempting to leave with what little dignity she could muster.

But Pete seemed determined to humiliate her. 'Hey, guys,' he shouted over the din, 'let's have a contest. Howard's Darwin bird against his Sydney one. I'll have ten dollars on the luscious Kate here!'

Kate pummelled him with her fists, trying vainly to escape his vice-like grip. 'Let me go!' she screamed in tears, twisting and turning as he dragged her to the pool.

'The lady wants you to let her go, McCann,' came a familiar voice from behind her, and Kate turned her head as Pete released her to see Grig descending on the two of them, striding almost casually. She stumbled and fell to one knee. Her top was askew and she adjusted it frantically, covering herself from the prying eyes that seemed to bore holes in her skin.

'Well, well, if it isn't old Grig! What are you doing here? Rescuing damsels in distress? Or have you a special interest in this one?' Pete asked sarcastically.

'That's enough, Pete,' Grig retorted, in a low tone that barely disguised his disgust.

'No, it isn't,' Pete grinned. 'The lady doesn't need rescuing. We were going to introduce her to the finer points of Darwin life, and if you hadn't interrupted, she'd have enjoyed every minute of it. So why don't you crawl back into your hole and leave us alone to enjoy ourselves?'

'You're asking for a few loose teeth, Pete. And if you weren't so bloody drunk, I'd give them to you,' Grig told him, in a voice laden with menace.

'Grig, it's all right,' Kate muttered, pulling at his arm. 'Just take me home.'

'*You*, go and get your clothes.' His tone was the coldest Kate had ever heard. 'Then get to the car and stay there.'

She pushed through the crowd, tears misting her eyes. There was a gasp, and she turned to see Pete take a swing at Grig, growling as he did, 'So our whiter-than-white Miss Kate isn't so white after all?'

Grig grabbed him by the shoulder and held him at arm's length. 'Don't say any more Pete, or I'll forget you're a fellow officer and drunk,' he spat, pushing Pete to the ground.

'Don't let that bother you,' Pete retorted. 'It's pretty obvious who's looking after her while Howard's away. Tell me, Grig, is she as good as she looks?'

Kate saw Grig stiffen, then in one fluid movement, pick the fallen man from the ground and carry him like so much garbage through the crowd that seemed to part by magic, to the pool.

'Cool off,' he said, dropping him in.

Kate fled upstairs. She grabbed her still damp dress and rushed headlong to the waiting car. Clutching her clothes in shame, she clambered in, turning her head away so he wouldn't see the tears.

Grig drove silently, concentrating on the road, leaving her alone with her thoughts. Huddled in the passenger seat, her wet hair drying in the breeze, Kate felt sorry for herself. Nothing made sense any more. All the hints and insinuations she had heard since she arrived now came together in her mind, and Pete McCann's drunken ramblings whirled relentlessly around in her head.

That Howard was not the man she had thought him to be was now patently obvious. She could hardly believe that he was involved with Nola. Howard had always said that Nola wasn't his type. She was too loud and flamboyant, and he liked girls with style. That was what he'd said. Style. Kate remembered laughing when he'd told her *she* had style. Now it was clear that style meant nothing to Howard if the other goods were more readily available.

What am I going to do? she asked herself. My whole life has ended up in a heap of broken dreams, and a lot *he* cares, she told herself angrily, looking sideways at Grig's stony countenance. It's all too much, too much. The sooner I get out of here and away from you and Howard the better off I'll be!

That she was thinking more of Grig's reaction than Howard's suddenly occurred to her, and she broke down and wept.

Here I go again, she thought, trying desperately to stop her sobs. Every time I'm anywhere near you for more than half an hour, she told Grig silently, I start to cry.

Grig ignored her sobbing, screaming the little car down a dirt track to the beach front. 'I'm going for a walk,' he informed her. 'If you want to come, put your clothes on, and don't open your mouth, or I'll forget you're a woman. Otherwise, stay in the car and don't move. If

you're not here when I get back, you can damn
well fend for yourself.'

Suddenly Kate didn't want to be alone as she
watched him stride on to the beach and disappear
from view. In panic, she pulled her still damp
dress over her bikini and hurried after him.

She saw him loping off into the distance and
had to run to catch him. She was glad she'd left
her shoes in the car; running barefoot in the sand
was soothing somehow. She decided not to catch
up with him, but to just keep him in sight. Just
the knowledge that he was there was enough to
still her raging thoughts and calm her aching
head.

After what seemed like hours, but could only
have been a few minutes, Grig stopped and she
caught up with him. She could see he was still
angry, furious even, and that the time had come
for recriminations and, she hoped, for explanations.

'You would have to be the most infuriating little
bitch I've ever had the misfortune to have to deal
with!' he shouted at her, as she approached.

'You don't have to shout,' she said unhappily.

'Oh, yes, I bloody well do! That's why we're
here. If I'd taken you back to the flat, the whole
neighbourhood would have heard what I thought
of you!' he continued at the top of his voice.

Kate turned on her heel and stalked back down
the beach to where the car was parked, leaving
him to yell at the empty air.

'Come back here, you!' he snarled, catching up
with her and spinning her round to face him. 'I
haven't finished with you yet!'

'Oh yes, you have!' she spat back, shrugging his hands away with an effort, yet perversely wanting him to touch her.

'Come back here,' he repeated. 'And look at me when I'm speaking to you!'

Kate spun round to glare at him. 'You're not speaking to me!' she screamed. 'You're shouting. So I won't look at you till you stop yelling!'

He grabbed her roughly by the shoulders and shook her. 'The only way I seem to be able to get through to you *is* to shout! It's a wonder I haven't done you an injury,' he snarled through clenched teeth. 'I've never met a woman who can infuriate me like you do! Though God knows how anyone can call you a woman. The way you've been behaving it's hard to believe you're even out of kindergarten!'

'Don't you speak to me like that! You've no right to. Just because you've kissed me a couple of times, it doesn't give you the right to run my life!'

'Someone has to. But thank God it won't be me. You're so bloody childish you shouldn't be let out without a keeper. I warned you about that party. I even tried reverse psychology in the hopes that your juvenile mind would rebel. But oh no, little Miss Teasing had to go her own sweet way!'

Kate reached up on her toes and swung her arm as hard as she could, catching him on the side of the face, leaving livid white marks on his cheek. 'You'll never believe me no matter what I say!' she screamed, shaking with rage. 'I hate you, I hate . . .!' Her torrent of abuse was cut

short by a huge hand that immobilised her head
and another that pinioned her flailing arm.

Grig carted her bodily to the ocean, waded in
waist deep, ignoring her struggles and cries for
help, then slowly and deliberately pushed her
under.

Kate surfaced, choking and spluttering. 'Cooled
off?' he asked savagely.

She battered at him, fingers clawed, trying to
rake his face. He ducked her again, easily. Then
suddenly, just as suddenly as he had grabbed her,
he let her go and waded away, to stand amused
and smug while she fought for breath and
balance.

Desperately Kate fought against her sodden
dress, trying to reach the shore before he did, just
to escape. Escape from this madman. But her
soaking dress was too much of a burden and she
collapsed at the water's edge, beaten and helpless.
She watched him stride towards her, the waves
making no impact and his hair like silver in the
moonlight. He looked like Neptune rising from
the waves, and her heart leaped.

His breathing was uneven, but his anger
appeared to be under control and her fear abated.
'God knows why I bother with you,' he said,
towering over her. 'I should leave you to wallow
in your own mire.'

'Don't touch me!' Kate wailed, in a small voice.
But her heart didn't mean it. Her heart was
crying *hold me, comfort me*. Everything had blown
up in her face and she rolled over in the sand and
pounded it with her fists like an hysterical child.

Grig's hand on her wrist was rough as he

pulled her to her feet, tugging her behind him to the high water mark. He hustled her to a large driftwood log and pushed her down on to it. 'Sit,' he commanded, the way a trainer speaks to a recalcitrant dog. 'What am I going to do with you?' The amusement in his voice was the last straw, and Kate broke down, sobbing broken-heartedly.

'Stop that,' he ordered. 'Your answer to everything is to cry, and it's high time you learned to deal with things without the water-works.'

'You'd cry too, if you'd been told what I was tonight.' She sounded contrite and sorry for herself.

'O.K., tell me what you were told. Or should I guess?'

'You'd never guess. And if I did, you wouldn't believe it anyway.' She sounded like a child playing a game.

'No? How about this, then? You found out that your ever-loving Howard wasn't all you'd cracked him up to be. In fact he and friend Nola have a thing going and have had for some time. Good enough?' he asked, with a sarcastic edge to his voice.

'You've known all along,' Kate cried. 'You let me make a fool of myself, and I suppose you've been laughing behind my back all this time, just like everyone else. I hate you, Grig Jacobsen, I hate you! I hate Darwin and Howard and the Navy and Nola and—and . . .' she broke down once more into incoherent sobs.

'For God's sake, woman, grow up! What did

you expect? You get engaged to a man you really
don't know much about, even though you've
been going out with him for years. Didn't it ever
occur to you to find out a bit about him?'

'I loved him. Why should I want to know
more?'

'You didn't even bother to find out about his
job, did you? What did you expect to do after you
were married? Sit in a flat somewhere and
vegetate? Anyone with a bit of guts would have
made the effort to meet his colleagues and tried to
learn something about his career.'

'Howard told me all I needed to know.'

'I just bet he did. Sounded great, didn't it? He
lied to you.'

'He didn't,' she answered, head bowed,
pleading silently that he would stop. For now she
knew the truth, but didn't want to admit it.
'Anyway, how would you know?' she asked,
trying to salvage a little pride.

'You as good as told me. He was a Sub-
Lieutenant here before he made Lieutenant. He
did his navigation here, just like the rest of us.
But if you don't believe that, you *do* know he lied
to you about Nola.'

'He didn't lie,' Kate whispered, still hanging
grimly to her shattered dreams. 'He just didn't
tell me.'

'That's splitting hairs, and you know it. Wake
up, kitten,' said Grig softly. 'You've been taken
for a ride. Maybe not deliberately, but you're so
damn naïve . . .' he broke off lamely.

'I'm so tired of being called naïve,' Kate
sighed, more to herself than to Grig.

'Never mind. It isn't such a bad thing to be.' His voice was so low she almost missed it.

'Why didn't you tell me?' she asked him, in a tone of regret.

'It wasn't my place to tell you. I'm sorry you had to find out this way, though. I tried to stop you, but then when you were so determined to go, I thought it was none of my business. But at the last moment I felt you might need me, so like Sir Galahad, I came riding to the rescue. It was just as well. Things got more out of hand than I'd anticipated. I had hoped to get there before anything developed.' He sounded sad, and Kate looked up to see him gazing across the moonlit water.

'You knew Nola well too, didn't you?'

'Yes. Nola and I have locked horns a couple of times. I saw her earlier the day of the exhibition and warned her off. But you know Nola.'

Kate's heart leaped. He'd tried to save her embarrassment, so he must care a little. Mustn't he? 'I suppose there's nothing left for me to do but go back home?' she sniffed, hoping deep down that he'd ask her to stay.

Somehow, knowing about Howard didn't affect her as much as she'd expected. But the idea of never seeing Grig again tore at her soul and made her cry again.

'Wouldn't it be better if you waited and sorted things out with Howard? He'll be back the day after tomorrow.' His voice was matter-of-fact.

'Is that the problem that made you angry?' she asked.

'Yes. But let *him* explain that. It will be better

if you leave here knowing exactly how you stand. Maybe then you can sort yourself out.'

'I suppose you're right. You usually are,' she gave him a weak smile.

'All right, then. Dry your tears and I'll take you home. A good night's sleep and everything should look better in the morning,' said Grig, putting his arm around her shoulders as they started back along the beach in silence.

He opened the door of the car for her, then leaned over to whisper confidentially in her ear, 'It's just as well it was me and not Howard who rescued you tonight. If you were *mine* when I found you half-naked, wrestling with another man, I'd have done more than dump him in the pool. I'd have have killed him!'

Kate's heart raced. 'What would you have done with me? That is if I were yours?' she whispered.

'I don't think I would have killed you, but I would have been tempted, and I'm sure I would have thought of a suitable punishment,' he replied.

'Oh!' she whispered happily to herself.

CHAPTER SEVEN

PANIC, blind panic drove Kate. Unsure of her feelings and certain that she could not face him, she ran. Ran from the man she'd told everyone was so understanding and kind. But now, after finding that he'd lied to her and cheated with another woman, she didn't know how she would react. She didn't know if she had the courage to face him with the truth, and she was too confused and shaken to even think about it.

Howard's phone call had come early that morning after Grig had left the flat. She hadn't expected him back for another two days. But she had a sneaking suspicion that Grig knew more about Howard's movements than he was telling her. Although, she thought, it was Grig who had told her Howard would return in two days.

Back in two days. Two days she'd hoped would give her the time she needed to sort out her jumbled emotions. Two days to decide if she still loved Howard and if the feelings she had for Grig were more than just an infatuation that would disappear with the return of her fiancé and normalcy. Two days to decide if she still loved him! More like two days to decide if she could overlook, in the man she intended to marry, what she'd found out at Nola's party. It wasn't enough time. Two weeks wouldn't be enough time. But the problem had to be solved and she'd set her

mind to solving it. Now the time was cut to
nothing. She couldn't do it. She couldn't face it.
Nor did she intend to.

She couldn't face Howard. What would she say
to him? She didn't even know how she felt herself.
She should feel disillusioned and betrayed. But
the only thing she felt was a strange relief.
Perhaps it was shock? She didn't think so.
Knowing Grig had turned her whole conception
of love upside down. I don't know now if what I
felt for Howard *was* love, she thought.

All she really knew was that she couldn't face
Howard. Not today. Not tomorrow. Perhaps not
ever. She needed time, and somehow, even if it
meant running away, she was going to take it.

Howard had told her on the phone that he
would see her at the flat early in the evening and
that he was looking forward to it. His voice had
been loving and just as she'd remembered it, with
no hint of doubt or apprehension. Kate was
certain that he knew nothing of the events at
Nola's party.

Her burning desire, now, was to run. As far
and fast as she could, from Darwin, Grig,
Howard and, she suspected, from herself.

The only thing she remembered of her drive
into the city was the confusion she caused at the
traffic lights. Her mind in turmoil, she had lapsed
into a state of withdrawal and hadn't noticed the
lights turn to green. The furious honking of
horns brought her back to earth with a thump. In
her confused state, she'd managed to stall the car,
which only added to the furious din, and she
arrived at her destination amazed at the command

of the English language held by some Darwin drivers.

She found a parking spot near the airline office, more by good luck than good management, and hurried distractedly into the building.

Her panic changed to dismay as she approached the ticket counter. Nola! The very last person she wanted to see at this moment. All the feelings of insecurity and unhappiness she had felt after the débâcle of the party came flooding back, and she had to hold on to the counter for support. She was tempted to turn and run. Run! That's all you've been doing since Howard phoned this morning, she told herself. It's time, my girl, that you pulled yourself together and faced a few things. And this is as good a time as any. You *will not* let that woman see how much she affects you.

So what if she thinks you're running away? It's none of her damned business anyway. She should be pleased if I am, Kate thought. After all, it will make it a lot easier for her. She'll have Howard all to herself after I leave and she won't have to lie about it either. A lot I care anyway. Kate hesitated, bewildered. I really *don't* care, she told herself and a weight seemed to have been lifted from her shoulders.

The look on Nola's face when she saw who her next customer was made Kate smile wryly to herself. It was comical. Confusion, embarrassment and a hint of fear flitted across the blonde girl's striking features. Then a veil descended over her pale blue eyes as she asked apprehensively, 'May I help you, Kate?'

Nola's usual strident tone was surprisingly

subdued, giving Kate an excuse to inject a hard edge to her own voice. 'I'm sure you can,' she said quietly. 'I would like to book my return flight to Sydney.'

'Surely you aren't leaving us so soon?' There was a note of hopefulness in her voice that didn't escape Kate.

Kate's reply was brusque. 'I can see no reason to stay. So I'd like to get on the first available flight.'

'I'm sorry, Kate,' Nola answered, and to Kate's dismay sounded as though she meant it. 'The flights are booked solid till next week— school holidays.'

Kate was stunned. The idea that she might not be able to leave immediately had never entered her mind. She paused for a split second to let the information sink in.

'It's important that I leave today,' she stated dogmatically. 'I'm sure with your connections you could do something for me. After all,' she continued, the bitch in her surfacing, 'I do think you owe me something, don't you?'

Nola had the grace to blush. 'Best I can do is put you at the top of the standby list.'

'Not good enough,' Kate stated, beginning to enjoy the effect she was having on her blonde rival. 'You see, my dear Nola, it's in *your* best interest that I leave today.'

Nola stared and started to argue.

'Howard's back,' Kate snapped. 'I'm sure you can see how many problems could arise if I were forced to tell him about your party.'

Nola's eyes widened in something like fear. 'Let me see if I can swing something.' She made a display of perusing her lists, then left the desk to make a phone call out of Kate's hearing. She returned, smiling and obviously relieved. 'One of the hostesses has agreed to postpone her return, so there *will* be a seat for you.'

'Wouldn't be you, by any chance?' Kate asked, and was inordinately pleased to see Nola flush once more. I didn't know I could be such a bitch, she told herself. Just shows what one has in one when pushed. And she sure pushed me! What's more, I could get to like being bitchy, she mused.

Nola took Kate's ticket and began to fill in the details. 'You'll be on the two a.m. flight, known to the locals as the "drunks flight".'

Kate couldn't help herself. 'Why the drunks flight?' she asked.

'Most of the passengers spend a few hours in the bar before take-off, then have to be poured into the plane.' Nola's explanation seemed to ease the tension and as she handed Kate the ticket she said hesitantly, 'Kate, about the other night . . . I'm really sorry . . .'

'Don't give it another thought, Nola dear. As a matter of fact, you rather did me a favour. Thanks for the booking. I'm sure we'll meet again somewhere. But I rather hope not!' Kate picked up her ticket and turned on her heel, only to be confronted by Grig's paintings, still on display behind her.

They drew her like a magnet. Slowly she moved past them, taking in their beauty once more, drinking in the strength and colour with an intensity that would imprint them on her mind's eye for all time.

She stopped before the brolgas, and tears filled her eyes. Mine, she thought. Mine, and I'll never see it again, or Grig. If I can't see Grig, at least I can have the painting. It's mine, he said so, and I'm going to take it with me. She touched it gently, feeling the textures of the oils. The 'sold' sign was still on it, but not her name. The other paintings had the buyer's name on them, but not hers. She wondered why it should be different. I'll ask them if I can take it now, she thought. Surely when they realise I'm leaving today they'll make an exception. They might even know how much it cost, and I can leave the money for Grig at the flat.

She knew that the impulse was irrational, knew in her heart that the painting would always remind her of places and events she should forget if she were to make a life for herself with someone else. But reason, she now knew, where Grig was concerned, had flown out of the window, days ago when he first kissed her.

All that seemed important now was to run back to the safety of her flat in Sydney, with this one reminder of a love that could never be.

She looked around cautiously, pleased to see that Nola had apparently left for greener pastures. And, before her resolve could vanish, she approached the information desk.

A young man was busily sorting papers as she approached and he looked up, smiling. 'May I help you?' he asked kindly.

Kate's courage almost deserted her and she mumbled the words she had been rehearsing in her mind.

'I beg your pardon,' he said politely. 'I didn't catch what you said.'

She cleared her throat and started again. 'I purchased—well, someone else purchased for me, one of the paintings on display. I'm leaving today and I was wondering how I go about getting the picture to take with me.' The words came out in a breathless rush.

The clerk looked surprised. 'I really am sorry,' he said, 'but the paintings can't be released until the exhibition is over.' He really did look sorry, and Kate began to have second thoughts about things.

'I'd really like to take it with me now, if I could,' she told him, pleading with her eyes. 'It's that one over there, the brolgas.'

'The person in charge should have told you and your friend the conditions of sale when you bought it,' the clerk said severely. Kate wasn't sure if he were angry with her or the person who had neglected to tell her the important conditions of sale. 'Still, if you'd like to wait, I'll speak to the manager and see if there's anything that can be done.' He smiled at her reassuringly, and Kate breathed a sigh of relief. Perhaps she'd be able to take it with her after all.

The clerk disappeared into another office, and Kate fidgeted worriedly. She lit a cigarette, something she seldom did in public, and puffed at it nervously, hardly even aware that it was in her hand. It was only something to keep her hands busy. She forced a bright smile on to her face when the clerk returned with the manager in tow and prepared to tell her story once more, rehearsing it in her mind so that it would come out without stutters.

The patent smile on the manager's face made her feel guilty—why, she couldn't tell. After all, her request wasn't really so unreasonable. She wasn't trying to steal the picture; Grig had given it to her. She only wanted her property, so why did she feel so guilty? Why did she have this impending sense of doom? You've got to get a hold of yourself, she told herself. No one can say you haven't got a perfect right to leave this dreadful town and take what belongs to you with you. But somehow it didn't feel right, and for the first time in her adult life, Kate felt she was somehow cheating, but who she was cheating wasn't clear, unless it was herself.

'Miss——?' the manager said, with a definite question in his voice.

'Rhodes,' Kate supplied.

'Miss Rhodes,' he continued. 'I'm terribly sorry, but I've just been speaking to Mr Jacobsen and he has advised me that the particular painting you mentioned is very important to the collection and he wants it to stay here until the end of the showing.'

Kate gasped. He'd spoken to Grig, now he'd know she was leaving.

'However,' he continued, in his 'keep the customer happy' voice, 'if you would like to leave a forwarding address, he'd be only too happy to send it on to you.'

Kate didn't know what to say. She didn't want Grig to know her address, and she didn't know why. But something inside, perhaps it

was pride, refused to allow him even that claim
on her.

'I don't know exactly where I'll be for a while,'
she lied. 'Perhaps I can send for it myself.' She
knew she was beaten and only wanted to make a
graceful exit.

Both men smiled knowingly. 'That's probably
the best solution, all round, Miss Rhodes,' the
manager said. 'Sorry we couldn't be of any
further help.'

'Thank you for your time,' said Kate, and left,
casting a last lingering look at the brolgas over
her shoulder.

Driving back to the flat, the events of the day
whirling round in her mind, she suddenly
realised that one very important fact had slipped
her mind in all her panic. Grig was still in
Darwin and now, after the airline manager's
interference, he knew she was leaving. It was
even likely that both Howard and Grig could be
at the flat together this evening, and that was a
meeting that she really had to avoid at all costs.
She had almost convinced herself that she now
could face Howard. Since her plane would be
leaving so late, it was almost inevitable. But now
that she realised that Grig could be there too she
knew it was impossible.

What am I going to do? she asked herself. The
plane leaves so late and I've nowhere else to go
but the flat. It's a mess, a complete mess, and I've
no one to blame but myself. It's all my own fault.
Why did I insist on coming here in the first
place? I could have stayed at home. After all,
Howard was due to come back South soon,

anyway. If I'd only been content to wait for him, none of this would have happened. And you would have ended up married to him, she told herself. A man you couldn't trust while he was away. But I wouldn't have known that. No . . . but what would have happened if you'd found out after you were married? Shut up, brain, she cried to herself, shut up and leave me alone!

She stormed into the flat, her mind a whirl of contradictions. For someone who had gone through life with very little in the way of emotional upheavals, her present predicament took on the proportions of a major earthquake. Not even as an impressionable schoolgirl had she felt the pangs of first love as so many of her friends had. And she had been the one giving out good advice and supplying a shoulder to cry on. Now, at twenty-five, when she needed the comfort of a close friend, she was alone. Alone, to solve the mysteries of love and to try to sort out her own tangled emotions.

Packing had to be her first priority. Then she would decide what she would do or where she would go until the plane left. She would have to find somewhere—somewhere where neither Howard nor Grig would be able to find her. But she couldn't find the energy to start and she collapsed into a chair, defeated.

She felt better, somehow, after she had cried out all her frustrations and confusion, and with a determination she dredged up from her inner core, began to prepare for her flight.

Each dress she pulled out from the wardrobe seemed to have a story to tell, a story that reminded her of either Howard or Grig, and her packing became a nightmare. The green jersey she had worn to Nola's party brought back memories of her confrontation with Grig on Casuarina Beach, and she remembered it was on that night she knew she loved him.

But now once more, she didn't know. She was sure now, at least, that she didn't love Howard. But good sense kept telling her that she hadn't known Grig long enough to love him. While her deeply hidden, romantic streak kept whispering to her about love at first sight.

Her packing was almost done and she picked up the beautiful red sarong that Grig had bought for her that first day. She smiled as she remembered his teasing in the shop and coloured at the memory of her attempted seduction in the flat's kitchen. She loved this piece of cloth now, more as a token than as a garment.

A friend was what she needed now more than anything. But of course, she had one. Sheila! Sheila would let her stay there until her plane left and wouldn't tell anyone she was there. She'd swear her to secrecy and Sheila would respect that. But maybe she would tell Grig. She was Grig's friend, wasn't she? No! She said she'd be there if I needed anyone, Kate recalled, and immediately felt her load lighten. I'll finish what I have to do and phone her straight away. With a lighter heart, she finished her packing.

The bedroom, scene of so much emotion, was tidy. Kate's bags stood ready at the door and Kate herself was ready to leave. She had just taken a final look around to see she'd forgotten nothing when the sound of the flat door startled her.

'Kate, Kate love, I'm back!' Howard!

She froze, then her heart began to pump frantically. Caught! Caught with no way out. Her mind raced, looking for some escape. But there was none. What am I going to do? she thought desperately. She clung to the door jamb, taking deep breaths and praying that her senses would return to normal. Slowly they did. The time had arrived, whether she was ready or not, and Howard had to be faced some time. So, she advised herself, pull yourself together and let's get it over with. At least it will be one less mountain to climb.

'Hello, Howard.' It sounded trite. It was trite. But in the circumstances, she could think of nothing else to say.

'That isn't much of a welcome for a long-lost fiancé!' Howard commented, a wry smile on his lips.

For the first time, Kate realised that his eyes didn't smile when his lips did. She wondered if it was just this once or if she just hadn't noticed before. But on reflection she knew that his smile was no different now than it had ever been. Mesmerised, she stood and watched him come slowly towards her. She couldn't move or speak and, frozen, she allowed him to take her by the shoulders and kiss her—kiss her long and thoroughly.

Nothing! Kate wasn't really surprised. She had to deliberately refrain from wiping the touch of his lips, his cheating lips, from her mouth.

Howard searched her face. 'Something wrong, love?' he asked, puzzled.

She turned from his grasp and moved deliberately to the room divider. 'No, not really. Would you like a drink?'

This was going to be hard. Very hard. And she didn't know quite how to begin.

'Kate,' said Howard, 'something *is* wrong. You're not yourself. Has someone done something to upset you? Jacobsen hasn't been being hard to live with, has he?'

Kate almost laughed. If Howard only knew just how close to the mark he was! But it wasn't only Grig. Howard was at fault too. She handed him his drink, and took a sip of her own.

'No, Grig hasn't upset me.' Liar!

'Well, damn it, tell me what's wrong!'

This is it. Tell him now or you'll never get it out. 'It's us, Howard,' she said.

'Us?' She was surprised to see he was genuinely amazed.

'Yes, us,' said Kate, beginning to become angry as she remembered the humiliation heaped on her by his so-called-friends at Nola's party. 'I've come to the conclusion over the past few days that . . .' she broke off, still unable to say the words.

'Come to what conclusion? Come on, Kate, stop beating about the bush!'

'All right, Howard. To put it bluntly, I've decided that I don't really want to marry you.' She turned from his accusing eyes to gaze out over the balcony at the water.

'Well! That's blunt, to say the least. Am I to be given the reason for this sudden change of heart?'

Kate turned to see him drop into the nearest chair. 'I'm sorry, Howard. If there'd been an easier way to say it I would have used it. But there doesn't seem to be any easy way, does there?'

'I suppose not. A bit sudden, isn't it? You seemed pretty set on getting married last time we talked. What's made you change your mind all of a sudden?'

The question was reasonable, and she sat down opposite him trying to frame an answer. But nothing she could think of seemed right. She couldn't just come out and tell him she'd fallen madly in love with someone else. Or could she? That would be the answer he'd expect. But Howard would know straight away who that other man was, and she didn't want him to know. She didn't want anyone to know. Besides, there was more to it than that. Even if she'd never fallen for Grig, she would still have found out about Nola. So really, she rationalised, Grig has nothing to do with this. The silence was electric and neither seemed able or prepared to break it.

Finally it was Howard who broke the deadlock. 'What do you plan to do now?'

Kate took a deep breath and tried to speak as calmly and rationally as she could. 'Well . . . I'm leaving for Sydney tonight. Or should I say tomorrow morning. So you'll have no need to worry about me.'

'Of course I'll worry about you, Kate. I still love you. You know that.'

'Do I, Howard?'

'What's that supposed to mean? You *know* I love you, and I think I always will.'

'Don't lie to me, Howard,' snapped Kate in exasperation, her innate sense of honesty outraged at the remark.

Howard stood up and began pacing the room, seemingly unable to look her in the face. 'I'm not lying. And I don't know why you should think I am.'

She sighed. If this were to be sorted out at all, it looked as if she'd be forced to break her half-promise to Nola. Though why that should trouble her was a mystery. Nola had never once considered her feelings.

'This is a very small place, Howard,' she began. 'People talk. And I've been here long enough to find out what's been going on.'

He stopped pacing and looked at her. 'Oh!' he said, then smiled, a smile of relief. 'Been listening to gossip?'

'I hardly call it gossip when it's come straight from the horse's mouth. I ran into Nola. She invited me to a party, and I went.'

Howard's face contorted with anger. 'I would have expected Jacobsen to have seen to it that nothing like that happened!'

'Nothing like what, Howard? I didn't say what happened. Apparently you're well aware of what goes on at Nola's parties, and from what I've gathered are one of the ringleaders at her little gatherings when you're in port.'

'Come on, Kate,' he snapped. 'You don't expect a man to sit around just because he's engaged. If you hadn't come here you wouldn't have known anything about the parties and you wouldn't be upset.'

'How true! I wouldn't have cared a great deal if it had only been some harmless fun. But to be told that it's common knowledge that your fiancé is more than a little friendly with another woman is a bit of a surprise, to say the least.'

The thrust cut home and Howard grimaced. He didn't deny the charge. 'But, Kate, I'm a man. What happens between Nola and me has nothing whatsoever to do with how I feel about you. Can't you see that?'

'No, I don't see that at all!' Kate spat, beside herself now with anger. 'How would you feel if you found out I'd been having a casual fling, for want of a better word, with another man?'

'But, Kate, that's different. I'm a man.' Howard was nearly whining now.

'It isn't different at all. As the old saying goes, what's sauce for the goose is sauce for the gander. Except in this case, Howard, it's what's sauce for the gander is sauce for the goose. I for one think marriage is sacred. I would expect to be faithful to my husband and I would expect the same of him.'

Howard smiled. 'But, darling, we're *not* married, and that makes all the difference. Now just let's forget all about Nola and start again. You know it won't happen after we're married.' He reached out to stroke her hair, and Kate flinched from his touch.

'No, we aren't married, Howard, and it's just as well. Now I know what to have expected if we were, and I'm not prepared to accept that sort of treatment. It's over, Howard. In fact, you'd better take your ring back.' She pulled it viciously from her finger and in her rage threw it at him.

The look on his face was all she needed to set her off into gales of laughter. Astonishment, dismay, wonder and amazement all vied for possession of his countenance. Amazement that his little, introspective Kate should have the temerity to question his judgment of the situation. That she should show a stiffer side to her character than he had ever dreamed she possessed.

She watched him through her merriment, aware now, that she had never really loved him. She had been awed by the attentions of her big brother's friend. She had grown up in the years she'd known him, but he hadn't. He was still a boy in a man's body—a spoiled, conceited boy, sulking if his plans were thwarted, dipping his hand in the cookie jar and crying when he was caught that it had not been his fault, but someone else's.

Kate felt she had to know why he had ever wanted to marry her in the first place. 'What about Nola? Don't you think that now you'll be able to make some sort of life with her? Surely you must feel something for her?' She watched his face carefully to see his reaction.

'Come on, Kate, you really don't think I could marry someone like Nola! She's totally unsuitable. Good fun, but totally unsuitable.'

'Suitable, Howard? Was that what *I was*—suitable?' Everything was clear now to Kate. But for her own peace of mind she had to hear it from his own lips.

'Well, of course. You have the right background and would make an excellent wife for a man who plans to make a career in the Navy. I hope you realise the chance you're throwing away,' he said peevishly.

'You're a fool, Howard,' Kate told him. 'One of these days I hope you grow up. I'm just pleased that I found out before it was too late that I could never have had children while I was married to you. I'd have been too busy taking care of you. And you'd be child enough for any woman!'

She was surprised at her own venom, but she realised on reflection that most of it had been stored over the years and came pouring out once the floodgates had opened.

'Now, if you'll excuse me, I have to ring for a cab.' She walked calmly into the bedroom and retrieved her cases, putting them by the door, and picked up the telephone to dial.

'Where are you going?' Howard asked. 'You have hours before your plane leaves.'

'I'm going to a friend's. I'll leave from there.' Kate continued to dial. But Howard snatched the receiver from her hand and slammed it down.

'I might have guessed!' he snarled. 'A friend! Now it's clear. You've picked up with someone else here in Darwin. I wouldn't be surprised if you're not leaving at all.'

Howard's suspicions were near enough to the mark to make Kate colour and he pounced on it. 'So I was right! Who is he? You didn't waste any time, did you? You've accused me of all sorts of things and now I find that you're not exactly Miss Purity. God knows what you were up to in Sydney while I was up here!'

Trust Howard to turn everything round to suit his own ends, Kate thought. Just shows how juvenile he is. 'Don't be so ridiculous, Howard. I'm going to a girl friend's house, if you must know, and I'll thank you to let me use the phone to call a cab.'

'Why can't you stay here?'

'I don't think we have any more to say to one another, and I don't think it would be wise to stay here with you.'

'You won't have to worry about me. I'm going back to the boat, so you don't have that excuse.'

Kate looked at him speculatively. 'Why are you going back to the boat? You don't have to do that on my account.'

'I'm not. I have to go back. We're expecting a refugee boat, and we might have to leave at any time.'

'I see,' said Kate, really not seeing at all, but not willing to get into a discussion of any sort with him. 'Still, I think I'll leave anyway.'

Howard's expression changed to one of furtiveness. 'Not afraid to see Jacobsen again, are you?' he asked, turning away so that Kate nearly missed the look of gloating on his face.

'What makes you think I'm afraid to see Grig?' Kate asked, trying desperately to keep her voice calm.

'Just a thought I had. Seems to me that you've found someone else, and the only man you've had anything to do with here in Darwin *is* Grig. If it had been someone down South, you wouldn't have come here.'

Kate blushed. There was nothing she could say. She could tell him that there was nothing between her and Grig, and that would be true in a way. But she couldn't tell Howard honestly that she didn't feel something for him. It had been Grig who had shown her that what she felt for Howard was not love, and for that at least she'd always be grateful.

She looked up from contemplating the carpet, to see Howard smiling at her in the way he used to when they first met—a smile that could turn any heart. But it didn't turn Kate's. 'Why don't you tell me the truth?' he asked gently. This was the old Howard, kind and gently, caring how she felt. 'You're in love with him, aren't you?'

'What if I am?' Kate asked, emotionally exhausted, and too tired now to fight it any more.

Howard's laugh was cruel and she saw the look that she'd thought was the old Howard back again had been a sham. 'I didn't think you of all people would fall for a fake like Jacobsen,' he sneered.

'What do you mean, fake?' asked Kate, her voice shaking.

Howard turned to the bar and she wasn't able to see the look on his face or in his eyes when he replied, 'He's nothing but a guy who got his promotion by influence. Didn't you know his uncle was an admiral? And how he's using his power for all it's worth.'

Kate blanched. 'What do you mean?'

'You really didn't think I was back here because of some piddling little refugee boat? Any of the boats could take care of that. I've been recalled—by none other than Mr High and Mighty Squadron-Leader Lieutenant G. Jacobsen!'

'Why?' The question seemed pitiful and inadequate, but there didn't seem to be anything else to say.

'Well,' Howard replied, 'my boat went aground out near T.I., and now I'm to be courtmartialled. Goodbye promotion for a couple of years at least and a great big black mark on my record.'

Neither heard the door open or see Sheila standing taking in the scene, as Howard continued, 'Jacobsen could have overlooked it. After all, most of the waters up here are uncharted. But oh no! He had to recommend a courtmartial. He's power-hungry, and by the look of it, this is a good way to get rid of me . . .' He never had the chance to finish.

Both Kate and Howard spun round at the sound of Sheila's angry voice. 'Why don't you tell the truth to the poor girl, Lieutenant Monroe? Or would you rather I did? I've come to the conclusion that you think Kate is a little lacking in brainpower to think that you could bring her to Darwin among Naval people and not have her realise what a lot of bull—sorry, Kate— you've been spinning her for the past God knows how long!'

'Keep out of this, you,' Howard shouted, 'or you and your husband will be sorry!'

'Try your bluff on someone else, Howard, it

cuts no ice with me. Get your things Kate; you're
coming home with me for the time being.' Sheila
grabbed the stunned girl's arm and, picking up
her handbag in passing, steered her out of the flat
to her car.

The two women were silent on the trip to
Sheila's house, and it wasn't until they were
sitting over a coffee that Sheila began to explain.

'I decided to come to see if you wanted to come
over here for dinner tonight and when I got to
the door of the flat I heard raised voices. I know I
shouldn't have eavesdropped, but I really couldn't
help it, and when I heard what Howard was
telling you, I just had to do something,' she
explained, a note of apology in her voice.

Kate was still a little stunned and her mind was
a whirl of conflicting thoughts. They tumbled out
in a jumble. 'How could Grig do that to Howard?
Anyone can make a mistake.'

Sheila broke in hurriedly, 'Listen to me. First,
Grig has no say whatever in whether Howard is
courtmartialled or not. Any captain whose boat
goes aground is courtmartialled.'

'But Howard said Grig was a Squadron- Leader.'

'All that means, my dear, is that Grig is the
senior Lieutenant here, so he gets a bit more
paper work to do. The decisions are made by
Navy Office and Grig just carried out orders like
the rest of them,' Sheila explained.

Kate's eyes widened and her mouth set in a
firm line. 'Then all that was just more lies that
Howard told me?'

'So you'd realised that he'd been spinning a
few?' Sheila asked.

Kate's eyes blazed. 'I've been coming to the conclusion over the past few days that all he's ever told me has been lies. And I don't think I've been getting exactly the whole truth from someone else I could mention!'

Sheila's laughter came out as a gurgle deep in her throat as she tried to suppress her hilarity. 'Grig, you mean,' she choked.

'Yes, Grig. And what's so damned funny?'

'You are. You're blind. Grig Jacobsen is head over heels in love with you.'

'No, he's not,' Kate answered quietly. 'He hasn't any time for me, so I'm leaving tonight. I was going to phone you anyway, Sheila, to see if I could spend the time before the plane left here, but you arrived before I got round to it.'

'He'll follow you,' Sheila broke in. 'Oh, not today or next week, but the first chance he gets, he'll come after you. In fact, it wouldn't surprise me if he put out an A.P.B. on you through his contacts in Sydney, just to keep track of you till he gets there.'

'He couldn't do that, could he?' Kate asked, bewildered.

The smile on Sheila's face was enough to tell Kate that he could and her words reinforced the feeling. 'You'd be surprised how much Navy guys can stick together, and how much information they can acquire, one way or another. Especially around Sydney.'

'Anyway, why should he? He doesn't care what I do or where I go. He'll be only too pleased to get rid of me. I'm only a damned nuisance to him, he's made that quite plain,' Kate retorted, a distinct quaver in her voice.

'Did he tell you that?' asked Sheila, mock innocently.

'He didn't have to. The way he's treated me since I've been here says it all,' Kate answered sharply.

'You two need your heads knocking together—you know that, don't you?' Sheila laughed, a loud uproarious laugh.

'There's nothing to laugh about, Sheila.' Kate was angry. 'You don't know what you're talking about.'

'Oh, don't I? Well then, tell me why, if he hates you so much, he should have come here last night, drunk as a lord and crying in his beer something about, "Dark hair that falls like a curtain when she shakes her head?"'

Kate blushed crimson, remembering all too clearly when he had taken the pins from her hair and ordered her to shake her hair down. She had just assumed that Grig had slept at the flat last night. She'd been so concerned about avoiding him that she'd gone straight to her room and had woken late this morning, assuming he had left for work as usual.

'He must have gone to the pub, I think, because it was pretty late when he got here. Spike took him to the boat in the morning. I don't know where he left his car,' Sheila mused.

'He didn't take it with him, it's still at the flat,' said Kate.

'He must have known he was going to tie one on. At least he had the sense not to drive,' commented Sheila.

'Was he all right?' asked Kate, a note of concern in her voice.

'Fine. Anyway, he was after he made it to the bathroom at three o'clock in the morning. We pretended not to hear him. But he was mumbling some very uncomplimentary remarks about you.'

'What did he say' Kate asked eagerly. She wanted to store up everything she could about him for the long cold southern winters she knew she would be spending alone.

'Thought you didn't care,' said Sheila, grinning widely.

'I'm only curious. It's nice to think the great Lieutenant Jacobsen suffers like the rest of us mere mortals—even if it is only with a hangover,' Kate replied, unable to look Sheila straight in the face.

'You really have got it bad! Admit it. Well, you can take it from me, so has he, if what he said then was any indication,' said Sheila, laughing again.

'Are you going to tell me or not?' demanded Kate.

'Of course I am, if it will keep you here and make life a bit more pleasant for Spike. Grig's been like a bear with a sore head since a certain lady who shall remain nameless arrived in town.'

The reference to Grig looking like a bear struck Kate as funny. She had often thought of him in those terms, and it sent her into a fit of the giggles.

'He does look like a great bear at times, doesn't he?' she gasped, trying to suppress the chuckles that threatened to turn to mild hysteria. She couldn't help feeling that the sooner she was away from his influence the better. She'd never been so emotional, weepy and hysterical in her life before, and of course it has to be his fault.

'I don't go in for the bruin type myself,' said Sheila. 'I much prefer someone a little less Herculean. About Spike's size, actually. That way, if he steps out of line, I stand a chance of knocking him for six. I don't fancy your chances in a knock-down brawl with Grig,' she grinned, looking Kate up and down mentally sizing her up. 'It would be a bit like Lionel Rose going a couple of rounds with Mohammed Ali,' she laughed.

Kate was beside herself with genuine laughter this time, trying to imagine Spike and Sheila in a boxing match.

'That's better. Now you're laughing,' Sheila said, obviously pleased.

'You're good for me, Sheila, you bring me back to earth. I feel much better now. But you still haven't told me what Grig said.'

'It wasn't much really, just some disjointed mumblings really. Something about a hazel-eyed, dark-haired teasing witch and a red sarong that wouldn't last long next time he saw it.'

'That could have meant anyone, and it certainly didn't sound as if he was too keen on seeing her again. Unless it was to wreak some sort of havoc,' said Kate, blushing scarlet.

'Come off it, Kate! He told Spike all about buying that sarong. He seemed to think it was a great joke making the shop girl think the worst.'

'He seems to tell you two just about everything,' Kate observed peevishly.

'Don't get green-eyed! We've been friends with him for a long time. He served on the same ship with Spike before he became an officer and they spent a year in the States together. Grig's never been one to let being an officer interfere with old friendships.'

'I'm sorry, I guess it does show. That's really why I've got to leave—to sort out how I really feel and decide what to do,' Kate answered slowly, obviously having difficulty in even admitting that much.

'Running away is going to solve absolutely nothing. And don't tell me you don't know how you feel—you're potty about the great lump. Mad, blind, hysterically potty about him, and from what I can see, it's the best thing that could have ever happened to him. I'd about given up hope of seeing him take the plunge. What you should do, my dear demented girl, is stay and brazen it out. What have you got to lose? It'll all come right in the end, you'll see.'

'I couldn't. I wouldn't know what to say or do,' Kate whispered, her voice breaking.

'Now don't start crying on me again,' said Sheila severely. 'You could always start by flashing your empty ring finger at him, so he knows that you've sorted things out with Howard and you're a free woman again.'

'But what would I do if he said he never wanted to see me again? At least this way I'll never know,' said Kate.

'I took you for someone with a bit more spirit than that. If you run away every time things get a bit too hard, you'll be running all your life.

Remember the words of our fearless leader, "Life
wasn't meant to be easy". And by God, it's not,
but you've got to grab every opportunity by the
throat and give it a good shake. Nine times out of
ten things work out. But in this case, I think
you're looking at a hundred per cent success rate
if you play your cards right.'

'What do you mean, play my cards right?'
asked Kate.

'Oh, just use a little bit of that feminine
mystique we're all supposed to be past masters at.
Haven't you ever conned a man before?'

'Well, no, not really,' replied Kate, amused
despite her misgivings.

'Where on earth have you been hiding all these
years? From what I've read lately, you youngsters
are supposed to be able to give us old ladies a few
tips, not the other way around,' said Sheila with a
wry smile.

'I wouldn't say you were that old,' smiled
Kate.

'Well, thank you, honey,' Sheila replied, aping
a Southern belle.

'Did you have to use your tricks on Spike?'
Kate asked.

'Of course I did. He'd never have got round to
it unless I'd pushed him a bit. You know what I
did? I sent him a Valentine with a marriage
proposal and told him it was a leap year. Before
he'd realised it wasn't, he'd said yes and it was
too late for him to back out.'

'Oh, now I understand what all the laughing
was about when Spike said at the barbecue that
you couldn't divide by four,' Kate laughed.

'Yes, it's become a family joke. But I don't mind, it worked and that's what matters,' said Sheila.

'But that doesn't really help me much. I can't send Grig a card, it's the wrong time of the year.'

'No, of course you can't, but you can use the female brain you were born with. If you really want Grig Jacobsen, something will occur to you at the right moment. Mind you, it's going to depend on exactly what you want from him.'

'Sheila, I'd settle for anything,' Kate admitted. It was a relief to have it said. She hadn't till then even admitted it to herself. But now that it had been said, she knew it was true and she would have anything he was prepared to allow her, no matter how little.

'That sounds very modern, Kate love,' Sheila grinned. 'But I don't think you'll have too much to worry about. Beneath all that bluff, Grig's really pretty conventional and I can't see him settling for anything less than marriage where you're concerned. Even if it is just from a chauvinistic need to make sure no one else gets a look in.'

Kate thought for a moment. 'I suppose I could change my plane ticket, couldn't I?' she asked hesitantly. 'Maybe I should stay for another day or two. Just to see . . .'

'Why bother?' asked Shiela. 'It's four o'clock now, and you've got till two a.m. to sort things out one way or another. If they don't work—well, at least you'll have tried.'

'But what can I do in that time? I don't even know if I'll see Grig before the plane leaves. And if I did, I'd probably just spoil things by bursting into tears.'

'Stop being so defeatist, my girl! Of course you'll see him. Just let me make a phone call to my dear husband. Then you're going back to the flat to cook a romantic dinner, and, I would suggest, change into that damned red sarong.'

'But . . . but . . . Howie?' Kate blurted. There was, she knew, no way she wanted ever to see her former fiancé again, especially in connection with the current scheme.

'Oh, bother Howie,' Sheila snapped. 'He's going to be too busy with that boatload of refugees tonight, but I'll be coming with you anyway, and if he turns up this afternoon I'll throw him out myself!'

And she would have, Kate realised, although when the time came, no such action was necessary.

CHAPTER EIGHT

THE table looked elegant, Kate decided as she surveyed the results of their efforts. In a whirlwind two hours Sheila had brought Kate and what she referred to as a box of 'seduction material' back to the flat. Kate had blushed, then giggled at the wry but amusing remark. Kate's smiles had set Sheila to laughing and it took a while for the two of them to calm down sufficiently to set Sheila's scheme into motion.

Sheila sent Kate into the kitchen with strict instructions 'to get on with it', while she set the scene. And, still not certain that anything would come of the ploy, Kate obeyed.

Now, with Sheila gone in a flurry of good wishes and last-minute instructions, Kate stood back and looked around at the final results of their careful planning.

Marinating drunkenly in wine, two huge steaks sat happily in the refrigerator, along with a very attractive-looking green salad. A hurriedly purchased pâté had been transformed, with the help of some crisp salad greens, capers and a bit of imagination, into a reasonably presentable entrée. A mango sorbet, that Kate prayed would be ready in time, was chilling in the freezer.

Two bottles of wine, one white, one red, were chilling in the fridge, along with a rather expensive bottle of Asti Spumante. Kate commented to Sheila that red wine should be served at room temperature, which set Sheila laughing once more.

'Room temperature in Melbourne, love, is fridge temperature in Darwin,' Sheila had grinned.

Displayed, Kate thought rather too prominently, on the room divider, was Sheila's bottle of Courvoisier and two brandy balloons. She moved them to a more inconspicuous spot, thinking as she did, 'My God! It will look as though I'm trying to get him drunk. Talk about female liberation! This is really taking it to its logical conclusion!' She smiled to herself at the thought of it.

'If it works for a man, I suppose it should work for a woman,' she mused, half seriously. 'That is if he comes. And if he comes, if he stays. Oh, hell! There are too many "ifs". If, another one, it hadn't been for Sheila, I wouldn't be trying this hare-brained scheme.'

She surveyed the table once more, admiring Sheila's handiwork. Sheila's tablecloth and matching napkins, Sheila's wineglasses and the arrangement of frangipani and hibiscus around the base of Sheila's candlestick, complete with candle to match the tablecloth. Kate glanced at her watch. Six-thirty—time to shower and change. Sheila had said Grig would be here by seven, though how she could be so sure, Kate couldn't tell. But she'd been carried along in Sheila's certainty and enthusiasm all day, it was too late now to start doubting her. At least it had filled in some of the empty hours today before the

plane, and if he didn't come, she'd at least have a
good dinner before she left.

And if she drank all the alcohol that Sheila had
thought necessary, it would be fitting. After all,
wasn't she leaving on the 'drunks flight'?

'I will *not* wear that sarong,' Kate vowed.
'Even if she has gone to all the trouble of pressing
it so it falls properly. He'd know immediately
that something was up. I just won't!'

On their arrival at the flat, Sheila, as a first
priority, had sent Kate into the bathroom to wash
her hair. Now it was almost dry and all it needed
was a good brush to turn it once more into the
silky midnight curtain that Grig had buried his
face in. Kate's eyes became warm and soft as she
remembered. She shrugged the thought aside
hastily. Sheila had been insistent that she wear it
loose. But Kate was determined that in this at
least, Sheila wouldn't get her way. 'I'll put it up,'
she decided. 'If I dressed normally, he might just
believe this is only a farewell dinner. But . . .' She
refused to dwell on what might happen if he
thought that everything had been planned with
an ulterior motive.

'I'm a fool to have let her talk me into this,'
Kate told herself. 'It will never work. And I'll be
on the plane tonight with another bad memory to
tear me apart. Not to mention a hangover!'

Tears welled in Kate's eyes and she dashed
them aside angrily. 'Well, my girl, nothing
ventured, nothing gained, as the old saying goes.
Might as well be hung for a sheep as a lamb. A
stitch in time saves nine. Stop being childish,' she
chastised herself as she realised that her mind was

behaving irrationally. 'If you really don't want to go through with this all you have to do is pick up your bags and take a taxi to the airport, *now*.'

Kate stood for a moment deep in thought. Then with a shrug she turned and hurried into the bedroom.

The red sarong was draped carefully across the bed where Sheila had left it and beside it, a clean pair of bikini briefs. But no bra! Kate grinned. Sheila was sure determined! But her plan was going to be slightly altered from here on in.

Looking round, she saw her suitcases neatly stacked in the corner. She pulled out the one she knew contained the dress she wanted and tossed it on to the bed. 'Damn!' she thought as she tried to open it. 'I forgot I'd locked them.' Annoyed at her own forgetfulness, she hurried into the living room for her handbag and scrabbled through it.

A frown creased her brow as she searched her bag. Where was her keycase? She tipped the contents of the bag on to the bed. No keys! Where on earth was that keycase? She knew she'd put it in her bag. But it wasn't there now.

There wasn't time now to hunt for the confounded thing. Angrily she scooped the debris from the bed back into her bag and replaced the suitcase with the others. It looked as though Sheila would get her way after all!

Snatching up her make-up and toilet bags from the dressing table, Kate hurried into the bathroom.

Fifteen minutes later she was ready, sarong draped carefully and make-up perfect. But she'd defied Sheila's instructions and piled her hair up in a knot on top of her head, only allowing a couple of wisps to escape over her ears and drape gracefully across her bare shoulders.

Her lipstick was the same bright scarlet as the sarong and she smiled, remembering how she had bought it on impulse just to match, after their day out. That had been a lovely day, she mused. But her musings were interrupted by the strident buzzing of the phone.

'All set, love?' Sheila's melodic voice cooed, when Kate answered.

'I guess so ... Sheila, I'm scared,' Kate whispered.

'Too late for that now,' Sheila laughed. 'He's on his way. Spike's dropping him off now on his way home. There was a small problem on board that held them up for a while. Spike just rang to say they were leaving.' She laughed again. 'Good luck! Oh, by the way, I seem to have picked up your key case by mistake,' Sheila's laugh rang out once more, followed by the beep, beep of the phone as she hung up.

'Bitch! Bitch! Bitch!' Kate fumed. 'And I thought I could trust her!' Her anger brought colour to her cheeks and a sparkle to her eyes. She was debating with herself whether or not to attack her case with a sharp object when the door opened and he was there.

Kate looked up and her breath caught in her throat. He was dressed exactly as he had been the first time she'd seen him at the airport. 'God!' she thought, 'why does it seem as if he takes all the oxygen out of the air when he comes near me so I can't breathe?'

'Hello, Grig,' she managed breathlessly.

He looked her up and down, that familiar sardonic look in his eye that made her feel even smaller than she was.' I didn't expect to see *you* here,' he drawled. The emphasis he placed on the word 'You', made Kate cringe. 'Thought you'd be out on the town, now Howard's back. Oh I forgot. Howard's out chasing refugees, isn't he? Waiting for someone else? Pete McCann, perhaps?' he asked sarcastically.

Kate's eyes blazed. 'You know damned well I'm leaving tonight. They told you at the airline office when I asked if I could have my painting.'

Grig's lips set in a sneer. 'Of course—how stupid of me! Howard must be very annoyed with you to send you back before you've had any time together. What happened? Did someone tell him about your little escapade at Nola's party?'

'If you must know,' Kate replied heatedly, 'I did.'

Grig's lips twitched in a genuine smile. 'Silly, Kate, silly. You ought to know not to tell the man you intend to marry about things like that. It could make him *very* angry.'

Kate's hands clenched at her sides and it took all her strength of will to keep them there. She wanted to hit out at him, hurt him as she was hurting. Instead she took a deep breath and said, almost calmly, 'Howard and I won't be getting married. I gave him his ring back this afternoon.' The only sign of her agitation was the heaving of her breast.

'What a pity,' he said scathingly. 'I was looking forward to being at your wedding. Never mind, there's always the chance that you'll invite me when you *do* manage to get someone to the altar.'

Kate was speechless. The audacity of the man. The sheer audacity!

'I don't know what you'd planned for tonight,' he continued, ignoring Kate's blazing eyes and obvious anger. 'But I'm starving, so you might as well make yourself useful and make us both something to eat while I have a shower. You'll need to eat before you travel,' he added, his voice losing some of its hard edge.

Kate moved away so that Grig could see the table. With an effort she swallowed the angry words that rose to her tongue and instead said softly, 'I already have. I was hoping you wouldn't have anything planned tonight. This is a farewell dinner—to thank you for taking care of me for the last few days.' Try as she might, she couldn't keep the sarcasm from her voice, and Grig caught it and grinned.

'Very nice,' he said, acknowledging the table. 'Someone will have to take you to the airport, and since I picked you up, it will be poetic if I see you off. Won't it?' he asked, watching her carefully. 'I just hope you've something more suitable than *that* to travel in,' he finished, looking at her sarong, before turning on his heel and disappearing into his own bedroom.

He doesn't care! He doesn't care! Kate cried frantically to herself. Oh, why did I let Sheila talk me into this? She pulled at the sarong in agitation as she wandered aimlessly into the kitchen, her mind in a whirl. Automatically, hardly aware of what she was doing, she began to prepare the dinner. The well-remembered tasks calmed her, soothing her jangled nerves.

Her heart jumped painfully when Grig's deep growl interrupted her heart-searching. 'Something smells good,' he commented drily.

Kate spun round to see him casually adjusting his own sarong as he watched her. She flushed and turned away so he couldn't see. Why did he have to wear that? she moaned to herself. Is he trying to tell me he knows what's going on?

'There's wine in the fridge if you want it,' she snapped, busily fussing with the grill.

She didn't have to turn to know that he was right behind her, she could feel his presence as clearly as if he had actually touched her.

'Of course we'll have wine,' he growled. 'This is a celebration, isn't it?' She heard the fridge open but didn't turn round. 'Pretty expensive array for a goodbye to someone you don't have much time for. You must be very pleased to be seeing the back of me.' The sarcasm hit Kate like a hammer blow.

It took all her self-control to answer calmly, 'Who says I can't stand the sight of you?'

'Well, you haven't said it in so many words, I must admit,' he answered, opening the bottle of red wine. 'But it's definitely the impression I've been getting lately.'

'Oh!' was all Kate could say. Satisfied that the steaks could take care of themselves for a while, she followed him to the table, silently accepting the wine he poured for her and just as silently picking at her pâté. The silence was intense until he broke it suddenly.

'Howard has been saying that he broke the engagement.'

'Oh!' said Kate, surprised.

'Yes. He seems to think you've been less than discreet since you've been here.'

'Oh!'

'My God, woman! Is that all you can say, "Oh"? I've had more intelligent conversations with six-year-olds!' he burst out angrily.

'Well, what did you expect me to say? One minute you tell me you don't know that Howard and I were through and the next you tell me you've known before you got here!' Kate stormed, throwing down her napkin and flouncing off into the kitchen.

Grig followed her and stood in the doorway watching as she put the steaks on to the plates and retrieved the salad from the fridge. 'That was stupid of me, but I wanted to give you the chance to save face if you wanted to.'

'You mean you expected me to give you some cock and bull story. In fact to lie? I thought you knew me better than that.' Kate wasn't angry now, just sad. Sad that he thought she wouldn't have the courage to face things as they really were. 'Anyway,' she added quietly, 'if Howard wants to tell people that, who am I to contradict him? The people that mean anything to me up here know the truth, and that's all I care about.'

Grig took the salad bowl from her hands and she followed him back to the table with the plates. He began to laugh as he helped himself to the salad.

Kate banged his plate down in front of him.

'That's right, laugh! It's the last time you'll get a chance to laugh at my expense!'

His murmur was just loud enough for Kate to hear. 'That remains to be seen.' But before she could reply, he changed the subject abruptly, demanding, in his usual arrogant way. 'What are you planning to do now?'

Kate felt defeated. What was the point to all this petty wrangling? He had no time for her, and if she was sensible, she'd accept that and cut her losses. The only thing for it now was to try to get through this evening with some degreee of civility, and it was obviously up to her to achieve that. She sighed deeply, then taking herself in hand, answered quietly, 'I've decided to go back to the hospital where I used to work.' Part of the anger she was trying so desperately to conceal, escaped. 'If it's any of your business.'

His eyes seemed to soften and Kate wondered if it were just the candlelight. 'What makes you think you'll be able to walk into a position just like that?'

She looked at him in surprise. 'They told me when I left that there would always be a job for me there if I wanted one. So I'm just taking them up on the offer.'

'I suppose they'll sack someone to give you a job?' Grig asked in a monotone.

Kate was genuinely dismayed. She hadn't thought that far ahead, and the idea of taking someone else's position appalled her.

'No ... No, that wouldn't happen. There's always someone sick or on holiday in a hospital, and I can relieve until a position becomes available,' she said hesitantly.

'Oh!' Grig appeared stuck for words.

Kate tried desperately to justify her stand, not knowing quite why she felt she had to, 'There's always plenty of specialling available for trained nurses anyway.'

'Oh!'

'And besides, I really don't have to work for a little while yet. I've still got enough money saved up to see me through for a few months.'

'Oh!'

'Now who's making brilliant conversation?' she asked, and for the first time that evening the tension between them eased and they both laughed as though it were the funniest thing they'd ever heard.

Still chuckling a little, Kate picked up the empty dinner plates and took them into the kitchen, returning with the mango sorbet, which had set beautifully.

'Very nice,' Grig commented, after the first mouthful. 'But it needs a little something . . .' He left the table and returned a moment later with the bottle of chilled Asti. 'Seems a pity to waste it, since you bought it specially,' he said drily.

Kate could only agree.

They ate and drank in silence for a while—a silence that was companionable at last. Companionable like the silences they'd shared on their day in the bush.

Grig seemed to sense it too, and he looked up and smiled—that slow, crooked warm smile that made Kate's heart leap. To cover the effect his smile had on her, she cleared away the dessert dishes. 'I'll make some coffee, if you like.'

'Coffee would be nice,' was all he said as she hurried to the kitchen.

Some time later after the coffee had brewed and Kate had hidden in the kitchen, washing the dishes, she emerged, carrying the coffee pot and paraphernalia on a tray. Grig wasn't there. She looked around, dismayed. Then a movement on the balcony told her where he was. She set the tray down and with trepidation in her heart, went out to join him.

Fanny Bay looked like a great silver lake, with the pale golden globe of a full moon floating on the farthest shore. It was beautiful, and the scents of the sea and the lush tropical flowers that grew in profusion all over the city seemed to add to the enchantment. Kate knew in her heart that she didn't really hate Darwin. In fact, she thought it one of the few places she had visited that she'd return to without any hesitation, and she wished things had been different so that she could have had the time to see all the things she had been told about.

Grig turned to look at her and she turned her face away. She didn't want him to see the pain in her eyes. But he reached for her and turned her slowly towards him. 'Are you happy about leaving Darwin?'

She started. How did he manage to read her thoughts so easily?

She deliberately chose to misconstrue his question. 'No one is ever happy when a relationship that seemed secure goes astray. Are they?'

'You know that isn't what I meant,' he said quietly, stroking her jawline and sending shivers down her spine.

'We'd better go and have that coffee before it gets cold,' she said, drawing away from him.

He draped his arm around her bare shoulders in an apparently casual gesture as they moved slowly back inside. Kate's mind told her to leave the warm circle of his arm. But her heart and body wanted her to stay, and she pulled away reluctantly.

Grig watched her intently as she poured the coffee and handed him his cup. 'Aren't you going to offer me any cognac?' he asked, gesturing towards the Courvoisier on the divider. 'That seems to be an addition to the household,' he commented. 'The last time I saw a bottle of that was at Sheila's.' Kate glanced up at him from under her eyelashes. Did he know? But his face was impassive.

'Come to think of it,' he added, 'a lot of the stuff on the table looks vaguely familiar. And I know it doesn't belong here at the flat.'

Was he teasing her? she wondered. But nothing showed on his face. 'I borrowed some things,' she said.

'How were you planning on returning them?' he asked slyly. 'Or was that the price I was to pay for this lovely dinner?'

He was teasing her. How Sheila was to get her things back had never been mentioned, and in all the excitement, Kate had not thought to ask.

'Well?' he asked. 'Who does it all belong to? And where am I to take it to?'

'You won't have to worry about it,' she said, turning away. 'My friend will pick it up.'

He chuckled. 'How will your friend get in?'

'She won't have to get in, she'll come and pick it up while you're here, I'm sure.'

'Oh, it is a "she". And how will she know when I'll be home? As if I couldn't guess.'

'What do you mean?' Kate asked, spinning round to see if he were angry again. But all she saw was a happy twinkle in his eyes and the gruff humour in his voice told her that he was once more teasing.

'Tell me what this is all about,' he ordered, standing up and towering over her.

She turned away from him, but he pulled her back to face him. He tipped her head up with his finger and looked deep into her eyes. She tried to turn her head away, but he took her chin in his hand and held her face so she couldn't. 'Now, tell me what this is all about,' he ordered again.

'Just a farewell dinner, that's all,' she managed to say at last.

'Don't lie to me, Kate. Please don't lie to me.' His voice was harsh and thick with emotion.

Tears swelled in her eyes. 'Don't, Grig—please don't,' she pleaded.

'Don't what?' he whispered. 'Don't do this?' and his lips sought hers.

She tried desperately not to respond, but she was powerless and her lips parted with a will of their own, begging for the balm that would heal her wounded heart. Grig's arms tightened round her and he pulled her closer. Her skin burnt where he touched her and she moaned unknowingly, pressing herself against him.

Suddenly her feet left the ground and she was caught up in his arms. His lips left her mouth to travel over her face. For a moment she fought with herself, her brain saying no, and her heart crying yes, yes, yes! Then somehow knowing it was inevitable, she wound her arms around his neck and pressed her face into the crook of his neck as he carried her to the bedroom.

At the bedroom door, Grig stopped and put her back on her feet as he opened the door. Then taking her by the hand he drew her into the room. She had been so involved with the feelings that were flooding through her that she hadn't noticed that it was not her room but his that he had taken her to. She looked around in surprise and he smiled, whispering in her ear as he pulled the pins from her hair, 'Don't you know what it meant in the olden days when a man took a woman to *his* bed?'

Kate hid her face behind the curtain of her hair. Could he mean what she hoped, or was he just saying words? His fingers winding themselves in her hair pushed everything but her need for this man from her mind. His fingers traced trails of fire across her shoulders and down her neck to the soft swell of her breasts, and her heart raced as he fumbled with the knot of her sarong.

The crimson cloth fell into a pool at her feet and she reached up to twine her hands behind his head, standing on tiptoe to do so. Grig's lips brushed her forehead and moved gently down across her eyes to once more find her mouth. She

revelled in his hardness, pressing herself against
him, moaning softly.

Grig pulled away to look at her intently,
stroking the soft dark silkness of her hair away
from her face. 'You're a wanton woman,' he
whispered gruffly. The words penetrated Kate's
emotion-charged haze. She shuddered involuntarily and her arms dropped to her sides.

The 'wanton' buzzed round in her head. Her
heart froze and she only wanted now to get
away—away somewhere, anywhere. She stooped
to scoop up her sarong and held it over her
nakedness, head bent and face hidden.

'Darling! Darling kitten, what's wrong?' Grig's
voice was soft and full of bewilderment.

She pulled away from him and turned pulling
the scarlet cloth around herself. But his hands on
her shoulders stopped her flight. 'Tell me what's
wrong Kate. Don't run away before you tell me
what I've done.' She realised that he was
pleading now and she stopped.

'You called me wanton,' she whispered
brokenly, and heard his quiet chuckle.

'Turn round and look at me,' he ordered,
turning her with his hands on her shoulders.
'Now, look at me,' he told her again when she
kept her head bowed. He tipped her head up with
a finger under her chin and she was forced to look
into the deep blue eyes that could see into her
soul. 'Yes, I called you wanton. But I didn't
mean to hurt you.'

'Then why did you say it? I'm only wanton with
you,' Kate whispered, closing her eyes. She didn't
want him to see the hurt and confusion there.

'I know that, kitten. That's why I said it. I like you being wanton with me.'

Kate's eyes opened in surprise to see his eyes sparkling with fun. He bent down to brush her lips with his mouth, whispering as he did, 'You can be as wanton as you like with me. But God help you if I find you being wanton with anyone else!' Then the sarong fell to the floor once more as he folded her into his arms and kissed her with an intensity that took her breath away.

Without really knowing or caring how she got there, Kate felt him place her on the bed. She opened her eyes wide as he pulled away from her and watched as he dropped his own sarong to the floor. He bent over to kiss her once more and, winding her arms around his neck, she pulled him fiercely to her. 'I love you,' she whispered before his lips took possession of hers.

The touch of his hands was electric and Kate tingled with excitement and anticipation. At last she was going to know what it felt like to be possessed by a man—a man she loved to distraction. He still hadn't said he loved her, but somehow it didn't matter. All that mattered at this moment was for him to soothe the aching longing in her heart and quench the fire in her veins. Only he could do it. Only his body could satisfy her. Only his lips could tame the raging emotions that threatened to send her mad.

'Love me—please, Grig, love me!' she cried, burying her head in the crook of his neck.

'Always, darling,' he moaned. 'I'll always love you.' The words seemed to come from another sphere, another place. But Kate knew at last that he loved her when he cried, 'I love you. I love you!' as they became one and the world was lost to her in the magic of his body.

The Top End sun burst over the horizon, spilling molten gold over the land. The little glade surrounded by marshland started to come alive with the arrival of the sun. Birds woke and twittered and cried their warnings to one another at the sight of the intruders.

The trees sparkled with the yet to be dried-out dew and the air was fresh seemingly washed just for the occasion.

Kate gazed round. How she loved this place! As her gaze took in the beauty of the place she saw a movement just outside the glade.

'Oh—Grig, look!' The brolgas had picked this spot to perform their ritual mating dance and nothing else could have been more fitting.

Grig took her hand, 'Ready?' he asked, smiling at the picture she made in her red sarong. A scarlet hibiscus was tucked behind her ear and her hair hung down across her shoulders.

Kate turned and handed Sheila her small bouquet of frangipani, and smiled to see that Sheila was crying softly clinging to Spike's arm.

The next few minutes passed in a daze of happiness for Kate and all she could remember was the azure blue of Grig's eyes. Until the soft melodic voice of the marriage celebrant broke into her reverie. 'Do you, Kate, take this man . . .'

'Yes, oh yes!' Kate's heart sang with joy.

Take 4
Exciting Books
Absolutely
FREE

Love, romance, intrigue... all are captured for you by Mills & Boon's top-selling authors. By becoming a regular reader of Mills & Boon's Romances you can enjoy 6 superb new titles every month plus a whole range of special benefits: your very own personal membership card, a free monthly newsletter packed with recipes, competitions, exclusive book offers and a monthly guide to the stars, plus extra bargain offers and big cash savings.

AND an Introductory FREE GIFT for YOU.
Turn over the page for details.

As a special introduction we will send you four exciting Mills & Boon Romances Free and without obligation when you complete and return this coupon.

At the same time we will reserve a subscription to Mills & Boon Reader Service for you. Every month, you will receive 6 of the very latest novels by leading Romantic Fiction authors, delivered direct to your door. You don't pay extra for delivery — postage and packing is always completely Free. There is no obligation or commitment — you can cancel your subscription at any time.

You have nothing to lose and a whole world of romance to gain.

Just fill in and post the coupon today to MILLS & BOON READER SERVICE, FREEPOST, P.O. BOX 236, CROYDON, SURREY CR9 9EL.

Please Note:- READERS IN SOUTH AFRICA write to Mills & Boon, Postbag X3010, Randburg 2125, S. Africa.

- - - - - - - - - - - - - - - - - -

FREE BOOKS CERTIFICATE

To: Mills & Boon Reader Service, FREEPOST, P.O. Box 236, Croydon, Surrey CR9 9EL.

Please send me, free and without obligation, four Mills & Boon Romances, and reserve a Reader Service Subscription for me. If I decide to subscribe I shall, from the beginning of the month following my free parcel of books, receive six new books each month for £6.60, post and packing free. If I decide not to subscribe, I shall write to you within 10 days. The free books are mine to keep in any case. I understand that I may cancel my subscription at any time simply by writing to you. I am over 18 years of age.

Please write in BLOCK CAPITALS.

Signature _____

Name _____

Address _____

_____ Post code _____

SEND NO MONEY — TAKE NO RISKS.

Please don't forget to include your Postcode.

Remember, postcodes speed delivery. Offer applies in UK only and is not valid to present subscribers. Mills & Boon reserve the right to exercise discretion in granting membership. If price changes are necessary you will be notified.

6R   *Offer expires December 31st 1984*

EP8